The Priesthood of the Purple Buffalo

CHUCK MEASEL

ISBN 979-8-88851-068-1 (Paperback)
ISBN 979-8-89309-122-9 (Hardcover)
ISBN 979-8-88851-069-8 (Digital)

Covenant Books
11661 Hwy 707
Murrells Inlet, SC 29576
www.covenantbooks.com

In *The Priesthood of the Purple Buffalo*, Chuck Measel weaves together details from history with those of myth and intertwines the beauty of the natural world with the soul-numbing nature of the profit-obsessed work culture that exists behind most office walls. Remone, a real estate agent, after being rescued from a fall and unintentional baptism in a frozen creek, learns the ways of the Sioux and realizes the sacredness of the land he once would have destroyed for financial gain. Measel's story elucidates that when human beings live in harmony with the natural world rather than seeing it as a commodity, Mother Nature will bind us together spiritually—and that the past remains "a vital and active invisible presence" in our lives.

—Marian Carcache, retired faculty member in the Auburn
University Department of English and author of *The
Moon and the Stars* and *The Tongues of Men and Angels*

In his first novel, Chuck Measel writes a science-fiction page-turner that evokes the tradition of Robert A. Heinlein's *Time Enough for Love*. Remone, a latter-day Lazurus, is transported to a Sioux village in an earlier time for an attitude adjustment and spiritual makeover. *The Priesthood of the Purple Buffalo* is a very impressive debut from a talented writer.

—Jim Buford, board member and past president
of the Alabama Writers' Forum and author of *The
House Across the Road* and *Water Over the Dam*

In a blizzard, the buffalo never turn tail and run like other animals of the plains. Instead, they turn to face the storm head-on and charge through.

Acknowledgments

THANK YOU TO COVENANT BOOKS for their help in answering questions and keeping me on the right path.

Thank you to Denise Trimm and her workshops in their many incarnations. First at Samford and then the Hoover Library meeting with Anna Gresham, Barry DeLozier, Alex Johnson, and Lauren Denton as part of the Cartel. We shared in reading each other's works and our innermost thoughts. A lot of fun and an experience from which I grew.

The workshops continued for several years with Doug Bullock, Jennifer Walker-Journey, Michael Calvert, Barbara Gordon, Elizabeth Traywick, and many other people I would like to thank who read and gave me input when the storylines got crossed.

My debt to Pam Hundley for reading and rereading the changes is huge. She pointed out ideas for plotlines and added a female perspective to the book.

Thanks to Barbara Baites for counseling me on punctuation and historical fact-checking.

I am grateful to Jim Buford for all his work and in believing in me and also for finding the perfect person to edit my book, Marian Carache. Thank you for turning your editing eye on my work and improving it.

My passion for all things Native American comes from their deep love of the land as something sacred. For this, I thank a true friend and Buffalo brother, Jim Johnson. His inspiration and help with concepts such as the book's title has been huge. I feel my role is to pick up the baton in a relay race to further the message, "Honor Mother Earth and Father Sky, for you live on one and beneath the other."

1

THE FIRST ONE UP IN the morning, Remone unzipped his tent and tried to be quiet as he stepped out into the snow. Sunbeams lit up the trees and reflected brightly in the whiteness. Squirrels leaving their tracks in the powder were the only witnesses to the splendor of the morning.

Nobody is going to be getting up this early after last night, thought Remone. *I am going to take advantage of the quiet and go bag the big one.* He slid his rifle out of the tent.

The trails were covered with snow, so he used the mountain peaks as a point of reference to keep from getting lost. His boots left deep tracks in the slush as he trudged down to the frozen river. Searching the woods, he edged his way slowly along the bank.

Through the branches, he saw him munching on the leaves of a cottonwood tree, the big buck he was looking for. Remone looked through his gun scope and moved in to get a closer shot, but the deer circled the tree, looking for more food among the frozen branches.

Remone inched his way closer, concentrating on the prize. He heard a cracking sound and realized too late he had stepped off the bank. The river he thought was frozen solid was breaking under his feet. Down he crashed into the frigid water. His rifle sank into the mud at the bottom of the river as the current pulled him downstream. All he could see was a ceiling of ice over his head that he couldn't reach.

Oh God, this is it! I am going to die.

Remone followed the light, and floating upward, he willed his spirit forward. Brief glimpses of faces flashed in front of him, some he knew and some he had never seen before. They crossed in front of him like vapors. Moments of his life replayed like an old black-and-white movie projector left running at a family reunion. Separated from his body, he knew he was crossing over to the other side. He felt a sense of euphoria and sadness at the same time as he reflected on his life.

The floating slowed until he came to rest on an island of green grass and shade trees. His eyes adjusted to the shadowy figures who walked about. A person approached, a faint figure he did not recognize until he drew closer.

"Dad," Remone cried as he ran to him.

"Romey," his father answered as they embraced.

"It is so good to see you."

"Yes, it is good to see you too. My brother, your uncle Ed, is here also. He recently arrived. I know you were troubled by his death."

"Oh." Remone choked with emotion. "I am so glad. I was so angry when I heard the news he had been murdered."

"Walk with me," his father said as he backed away. He pointed to the waterfalls cascading down from hilltops. "It is a beautiful place, so peaceful."

Remone and his father walked on through fields of blowing grass. Remone felt a different sun warming his face as he asked his father many questions, and they talked about family and friends.

"Here let us sit down," his father said.

"You died so suddenly there was no time to say goodbye," said Remone.

"No man knows his time. If I had known I had a bad heart, I would have done something about it. It troubled me that I went so quickly that I never got to say goodbye to you and your mother. Many times I have watched you and tried to speak to you through your dreams, but you were not listening."

"I was distracted, chasing money and the desires of the flesh."

"The living are distracted, chasing the things that are not important. The temptations of the material world."

"That is true," answered Remone. "You have grown wise."

"All who walk the streets of paradise grow wiser. Do you remember when we used to go hunting? I have fond memories of us traversing the forest together."

"You taught me all I know about hunting. You were always there for me," said Remone.

"I watched you this morning as you hunted along the riverbank. If I could have warned you that the ice was too thin, I would have."

"But now I am here," Remone said with a smile.

"Yes, but only for a while. It is my task to tell you your life is not over yet. You are going back."

"No, I want to stay."

"It is okay. I will be waiting here for you when it is your time."

The light faded, and Remone felt himself being pulled backward. Like an engine slowly swinging into reverse, the speed grew as Remone's visions of heaven shrank and the pictures blew past. Then there was darkness as he felt himself falling back into his icy prison once more.

2

S UDDENLY, SOMETHING SMASHED THE ICE above him. An arm grabbed him and pulled him toward the shore. Once he reached the riverbank, Remone heaved his head back and threw up the river water, fell to the ground, and passed out.

The pungent smell of deer meat and sweaty skin hit his nose as he opened his bleary eyes to three figures. Fog rose from the water, blurring the landscape. Their identity remained unknown as the dark shapes moved around him. Slowly Remone's eyes cleared to reveal his rescuers were three Indians.

They looked like they were from another time. Dressed like pictures he had seen of the Sioux from the 1800s, they wore buffalo hides and carried bow and arrows. One had a deer fresh from the hunt thrown over his shoulder. Luckily for Remone, they had stumbled on him in his time of distress. *But where were his friends?* Remone's head thumped with a terrible headache that added to his confusion. He looked up the hill where they had camped and saw no one.

Remone groaned as he struggled to his feet and yelled, "Jimbo, Greg, David!" But there was no answer. The Indians looked at him as if he were insane. He called again but heard no answer.

He couldn't understand any of the words the Indians were saying as they yelled back and forth at each other. But even though he didn't know their words, he knew they were arguing—arguing about what to do with him. They grabbed him and tied his hands, pulling him along the trail by the river and herding him like an animal for a mile up and down the hilly path. They turned and drove the exhausted White man into the woods. He saw smoke rising through the air from their village. He smelled food cooking. All he wanted was something to eat, get out of his icy clothes, and rest.

The teepees lay next to the river, nestled in a valley where it gave them shelter from the wind. Remone watched as children chased each other with sticks in a game that looked a lot like lacrosse. Women gathered water and warmed their meals on the open fire. Braves sat smoking their pipes, laughing, and talking in their strange language. Remone lost himself in the moment as they walked into the center of the village.

But then a group of braves galloped into the encampment. One of them saw Remone, pointed at him, and started yelling. Remone tugged at the rope that held him as he tried to back away from the riders and give them room to pass. The Indian who had pulled him from the river grabbed the rider's reins and yelled back at him.

Remone was taken to one of the teepees where they gave him dry clothes. The leather garb was strange to him and did not fit well, but at least he was warm again. He fell onto one of the buffalo hides, exhausted from his ordeal and slept.

When he came out of the teepee, it was late afternoon. Young maidens giggled at the strange White man dressed in buckskin pants that dragged the ground. His dark skin, long hair, beard, and mustache looked different from what they were used to. Others stared at Remone with hatred in their eyes while still curious about what he was doing there. No one welcomed him. They went about their work, preparing their meals and gathering firewood for the cold night ahead.

How might I escape and go back to search for my friends? thought Remone. *I know they will be worried.*

The Indians placed no guards around him and let him come and go as he pleased. They didn't seem to care if he stayed or escaped. He scouted the woods, following the path he thought they had taken when he was brought to the village, but with no food or gun in the dead of winter, his flight would be difficult. And he had no idea where he was. No, he would bide his time until he knew more. Then he would sneak out of the village when he had his chance.

Remone would, in the days to come, learn that the brave who had pulled him from the river was Pinchot. What Pinchot lacked in size he made up for in agility. He was the best horseman in the tribe and master of the bow and arrow. He could shoot with great accuracy from his horse at a full gallop. The village called on Pinchot to lead the hunt when supplies were low, and he always came back with something to cook.

A brave of great discipline, Pinchot fasted frequently, seeking the path that the Great Spirit had placed for him to follow. He would disappear for days at a time to commune with the Sioux's god, Wakan Tanka. His animal sign was the black cougar. Pinchot believed he got his speed and coordination from the big cat. He felt that the cougar helped him in the hunt, especially at night.

At first, Pinchot kept the White man because he thought he might trade him for horses from the Whites. Maybe the White man would be a big prize and they would give many horses for his return. But the Great Spirit spoke to Pinchot in a dream and told him to care for the White man, for he had a destiny to fulfill.

Pinchot took Remone to see the shaman, Returns Again, because he knew English better than anyone else in the tribe. The shaman had learned English when he was taken captive while he was out on a raid to bring back horses. A troop of soldiers came upon the shaman while he was with the rear guard. The Crow Indian scouts held a grudge against Returns Again. They attacked the shaman as he held the Sioux braves' horses, knocking him out and taking him to their military encampment and on to Fort Laramie in eastern Wyoming.

His time at Fort Laramie gave the shaman time to study many White men and their languages. He stayed with the Whites out of curiosity, watching and learning, but he could never understand the White man's desire for power and material wealth. The pursuit of land, livestock, and gold consumed all their time, and they became enslaved to the things they owned. He found the Whites to be unhappy and spiritually lost. Despite his time with them, he remained undeterred in his pursuit of the Sioux way. He escaped and made his long journey back home to the Black Hills where he belonged.

Now an older Indian with a long train of white hair flowing down past his shoulders, he sat outside his teepee, warming himself and stirring a cooking bowl in the fire.

"See what I have brought to Returns Again," Pinchot said as he motioned for Remone to sit down. "The Great Spirit called to me to pull the White man from the river."

"I have seen this White man in my dreams," the shaman said to Pinchot, speaking in his native tongue. "I knew he would join us. His seed will become a great leader of the Sioux. We will test him and see where his heart lies."

"How have you come to be with the Sioux, White man?" the shaman asked in English that Remone understood.

"I don't know, I was hunting and fell into the river. He rescued me," Remone said, pointing to Pinchot. "I need to find my friends and my rifle. I lost my rifle when I fell into the river, and it was brand new. It cost a lot of money."

The shaman translated what Remone said so that Pinchot could understand Remone's words. Pinchot nodded his head as the shaman spoke.

"Those things are gone. A new path lies before you if you choose to travel down it."

"I must find my way back to my friends. I have to go back to my job while I still have one," said Remone.

"And did this job make you happy?"

He looked down at his feet as he shook his head. "No, I hated my job," said Remone as he realized he needed to be more careful with his answers.

"Your job has made you a slave of the Whites. To separate yourself from the White man's bondage, you must change yourself. Escape from the termite people who seek only to devour all they encounter. The Sioux way is your path to change."

The shaman watched Remone with a piercing intensity as he tried to figure him out. Not wanting to appear weak, Remone met the shaman's gaze, never losing eye contact knowing that what the shaman said was meant to test him.

"You have a strong aura of purple, the color of one who seeks wisdom. It bursts like clouds around your inner being. From learning to look at the auras, one can tell which way the winds of destiny will blow."

Remone was not sure he believed in auras, having never seen one, but he hoped to earn the support of the shaman and learn from his new friend Pinchot.

The shaman's words made an impression on Pinchot. As he helped the White learn his skills, he formed a friendship with Remone. He came to believe that Remone had been brought to them to be converted to the Sioux way. Pinchot took it upon himself to teach Remone the things that would ensure his survival.

Learning the language proved difficult for Remone. Pinchot would point at objects and pronounce the Sioux words so that Remone would know what these things were. But most of Remone's communication with Pinchot was done by signing, frowns, and yelling at him in words that Remone had yet to interpret.

Hunting with a bow under Pinchot's instruction progressed until Remone lost all of Pinchot's arrows. Pinchot showed Remone how to find the right type of rocks to chisel into points and how to tie them to the sticks they found.

"Yeooow!" yelled Remone as the chisel slipped, and he brought it down on his finger. Blood poured out and trickled down his arm, mixing in the soil and broken arrowheads.

"No," growled Pinchot as he grabbed the chisel. "Here, watch closely," Pinchot said as he pushed the rock into the ground and struck it with the skill that had come from years of experience. "Practice," he said, clearly frustrated with the progress of his pupil as he tossed the chisel down at Remone's feet.

An Indian maiden who had been watching nearby had mercy on Remone and patched his hand. She avoided eye contact with Remone as she mashed yarrow roots as an ointment and wrapped his hand with leaves to keep it clean. Remone thought, *She must just be shy.*

Then they locked eyes in a frozen moment as she looked up at Remone, and he was thunderstuck with the beauty of her dark brown eyes. He learned later her name was Amber Moon, for the moon had a golden hue around it on the night she was born. Her mother had died shortly after her birth. To Big Elk, her father, she was precious, but he knew nothing of the skills needed to teach a young girl. Amber Moon did as she saw fit and grew up to be more independent than other maidens in the village. Her beautiful dark brown eyes filled her smiling face, making her look more compassionate to Remone, especially while she held his hand and mended it.

After several months, Remone made progress but still struggled to learn the Sioux language. He went to see the shaman confessing his frustration. "How can I become Sioux when I can't speak your tongue?"

"You place too much importance on the language and not enough on what is inside," the shaman motioned to his chest. "Words are a great invention of mankind but fall far short of telling all. Those things that are most important are bigger than words. Be patient and the understanding will follow."

Remone thought about the shaman's words and took them to heart. Pinchot continued teaching Remone, and they developed a friendship in which one could often tell what the other was thinking. With a little patience, Remone felt like he had made the transition and could communicate his thoughts and questions to those in the tribe that would listen.

3

BEFORE THE SNOW MELTED ON the riverbanks and around the birch trees, Pinchot decided it was time to outfit Remone with a bow. He chose a young ash tree about the size of Remone's wrist that stood his full height. The bow was cut in the winter because the sap was up, and this naturally made the bow stronger and more flexible.

"A green tree is softer and easier to carve," said Pinchot.

He showed Remone how to peel off the bark and how to notch the bow at both ends so it would hold the bowstring.

"Knowledge is just as important as skill with a weapon," said Pinchot. "Knowing where to find game and what their habits are is of equal importance to mastering the bow."

Pinchot told Remone to build a fire, and after it was burning, Pinchot hung the wood above it, slowly drying it. The shaman, Returns Again, joined them. As it dried, they sat around the firepit discussing their philosophy.

"The key to living in harmony with nature is to live with the land instead of destroying it," Pinchot said as he poked at the fire with a long stick. "Living with the land, not apart from it."

Remone sat quietly as the shaman and Pinchot exhorted their beliefs on why the Whites had gone so far astray. He realized what they were saying was for his benefit.

"Not destroying and drifting apart from nature but putting it on the pedestal it deserves as part of the Great Mystery," the shaman said. "This is the reverence which makes the Lakota view the world as a sacred place and not something to defile."

"Man is no better than any part of Wakan Tanka's creation, for we are all one part of the whole," said Pinchot.

"We are all to be the caretakers of the earth, but the Whites show no respect for the way that has been shown. He has journeyed far from the path that was planned before the world was made," the shaman explained. "He has set himself in dominion over earth and sky. His power lust knows no bounds."

The Sioux see themselves as part of one world," said Pinchot. "The Whites see the environment as something to conquer, dominate, and control."

Like real estate developers who plow down everything before they build on a plot of land, thought Remone.

The shaman looked into the night with a faraway look in his eyes and said, "A tree must learn to bend in the wind, bowing down to the will of the Great Spirit. If it is too proud to bend, it snaps in the wind, its old bones broken into pieces on the ground, slowly returning to dust."

From the buffalo guts, Pinchot stretched out the sinew to use as the bowstring, drying it in the heat of the fire for a brief while and then taking the multiple strands and twisting them together to give the string its strength.

The next day, Pinchot showed Remone how to string the bow. Hooking it on the bottom, he braced his foot against the bow and bent it to hook it to the top. The bow sprang to life. Pinchot held it up, plucking the string to see if it had spring to it. It twanged out a note as Pinchot nodded his head affirmatively and said, "Good bow, now let's see how it sings."

Grabbing a quiver of arrows, Pinchot and Remone hiked deep into the woods on a path that followed alongside the river, still icy with melting snow. Bare trees made it easier to see a great distance through the woods.

"Skill with the bow is good, but recognizing the deer's footprints in the snow is crucial to finding food in the winter months," Pinchot said, pointing to the tracks in the snow. Continuing along the trail, Pinchot stopped and stooped down to look at a bare spot where there was no snow. "See what is here," Pinchot said to Remone. "This is where a deer bedded for the night, see how the snow has melted and the grass is matted down?"

Remone nodded his head in understanding.

"When the winter is deep and cold, when it is difficult for the deer to scrape away the snow to feed on grass, knowing where the cottonwood saplings lie along the creeks and riverbeds will keep you from hunger," Pinchot said as Remone's lesson continued. "For peeling the bark from these trees feeds the deer's young."

As Remone spent more time in the Sioux nation, he began to believe that it was where he had always belonged. A less stressful lifestyle with more emphasis on living life in a spiritual way made the most of every day. At first, Remone had said he wanted to become Sioux to go with the flow as he appealed to the Indians for their help. But now, he said he wanted to become Sioux and he really meant it.

Remone continued to learn under Pinchot's watchful eye. He no longer had a rifle, but Pinchot had taught him how to hunt with the bow. For Remone, it seemed a much better way to spend his life than being stuck behind a desk in his office. Deer were plentiful, and the brooks were alive with trout—a land of plenty and a hunter's paradise.

But Remone's presence only angered his adversaries in the tribe. "White dog taints our hunting ground being here!" cried Black Wolf as he railed against the White man. "Soon there will be no game to hunt for." Backed by his entourage of braves, he stirred up many in village against Remone.

As tensions mounted, Pinchot took Remone to the tribal council to see who would stay and who would have to leave. The council met in one of the only permanent buildings in the village. Built with trees, branches, buffalo hides, and mud, it formed a rectangular shape and was built to be larger than the traditional teepees and could host the whole village. The ceiling was high so that rituals, council meetings, and trials could be performed inside.

A chimney allowed a large fire to burn in the center of the room where the tribe gathered. The tribal leaders sat on chairs adorned with hides and antlers—the trophies of past hunts. The closer their seat was located to Chief Slow Bull, the more their importance in the tribe. The chiefs were easy to recognize by the feathers flowing down from their headdresses, worn for rituals, celebrations, skirmishes with other tribes, and, of course, tribal councils where they led and directed the council to vote on issues facing the village. Chief Slow Bull's headdress was the most ornate with a long train of eagle feathers signifying his authority.

Because of his years and wisdom, Chief Slow Bull was chosen to lead his people. In his youth, Chief Slow Bull had proven his courage in skirmishes with the Crow. Rather than killing his adversaries, he struck them in coup using a spear with feathers attached to the end instead of a spearhead, humiliating them with an act of mercy when he could have easily taken their life. As time passed, he rose through the ranks of chiefs to be the head of the tribe. Slow Bull had traveled among the Whites and could speak English.

"How has the White man found his way to the Sioux? Has the Great Spirit brought you to us? Or have you come to steal our land and women?" the chief yelled angrily at Remone.

Shocked to hear the chief speak English, Remone could only say, "I am here to learn. My skin may be white, but I want to learn the Sioux way."

"We will see who is red and who is not. Whether you are a mouse or man. We will see who runs from his own shadow and who looks into the sun and is not afraid to go blind!"

"I seek only to fulfill the will of the Great Spirit and walk as a true human being," Remone said as he searched for the words that would soothe the angry chief.

"If you let this White man stay, he will bring more Whites and their diseases," Black Wolf shouted as he presented his case to the applause of many of the Indians. "Their lust for gold will drive us from our land. They will take our women. We must kill him now in a way that his soul will wander for all time!"

"It has been given to me to teach the White man, Remone," said Pinchot. "It is my burden to make sure he does not stray from the path. His destiny is to become Sioux and walk the way of a true human being."

"We must end this now!" Black Wolf yelled as he leapt from his seat with his tomahawk and grabbed Remone. "I will take his head and then his scalp for a trophy."

But Black Wolf had talked too long, and Pinchot grabbed the back of his arm and wrestled the weapon from his hands. "You are not the chief! You do not speak for the whole tribe!"

Jumping to his feet, Chief Slow Bull shouted, "How dare you defile this council. I am chief, and you, Black Wolf, are banished from this chamber. Your voice will be heard no more!" And he motioned for several braves to grab Black Wolf and physically remove him from the room.

When the braves returned, Slow Bull exerted his will over the council. "I say the White man stays, but he is Pinchot's student."

Then speaking directly to Pinchot, he said, "Because you are one who is highly respected in the tribe, we will entrust you with this White, but make sure he does not make your words into lies. He must pass many tests to become Sioux."

"I will accept this as my undertaking, as I was chosen by the Great Mystery for this task when I found the White and pulled him from the river," said Pinchot.

"What says the council?" Chief Slow Bull asked the other chiefs.

After a reluctant vote, Remone was narrowly allowed to stay.

"Do not make the tribe regret this decision," Slow Bull said to both Remone and Pinchot.

The shaman approached Remone and grabbed him by the shoulders and, looking him the eyes, said, "You must go through many trials to know the honor of being called redskin brother."

Realizing that Chief Slow Bull had not exactly welcomed him into the tribe, Remone asked Pinchot later when they were alone, "What will I have to do to stay in the tribe?"

Laughing Pinchot said, "To become Red man is truly Remone's destiny, as he will offer up a scarlet blanket unto Wakan Tanka. The chief has given Remone a path to join the tribe. It is up to Remone to walk the path."

The Indians had raised many orphaned White children in the Sioux way, even when the Sioux were the ones that had made them orphans, but for a White to enter the nation as an adult was a different matter. This could only be accomplished through a series of trials testing the manhood, character, and stamina of the man.

Many of these rituals were no different than what the Sioux imposed on their own sons as they grew from child to brave. All were familiar with the rites associated with the Sun Dance, scarring the males and giving them physical proof of their transition to manhood. But for Remone, these tests could be more formidable, for he was an outsider, and the depth of his character would have to be tested thoroughly. The thought that they might enjoy seeing how far he could take it and how far his limits could be stretched had not yet occurred to Remone.

4

THE SHAMAN AND PINCHOT DISCUSSED with Remone the path that would lead him to grow in the Sioux way. "You will need help on your journey. It is time for you to begin your vision quest," said the shaman.

"What is a vision quest and where do I have to go?" asked Remone.

"To a place that is not far away but most Whites have never traveled to," said Pinchot. "The place you must journey to is within yourself."

"How do I travel into myself?"

"By entering the stillness that is inside you," the shaman answered. "The vision will pierce the veil that shrouds your destiny from sight."

"You must also discover your animal sign," said Pinchot. "One who will aid you when needed."

"How will I do these things?"

"We will help you," Pinchot said. "The shaman will be your guide just as he was for me."

"Know that it is through fasting and discipline that you will reach the level of purification needed to commune with the Great Mystery," said the shaman. "You can also seek the aid of those who have already crossed over to the spirit world."

Some of the braves had their vision quest by retreating into the wilderness of the Black Hills, but others strived for this insight inside the sweat lodge. To purify themselves, the Indians used a low wigwam over a pit of heated stones and sweet grass. When water was thrown onto the heated stones, it enveloped the participant in a hot steam. The Sioux considered this process of sweating out the body a necessity before they could be pure enough to hear the voice of Wakan Tanka.

Four days of fasting in the wilderness left Remone dehydrated and weak. Walking into a part of the valley that was more desolate, he realized he had strayed from the path and lost his way. If he did not come up on one of the creeks and get some water soon, he felt like he was going to pass out. The sun was unrelenting as it burned his skin.

I need to pull myself out of this ravine and get to the top of this ridge, thought Remone. *Maybe then I will be able to see a creek or river.* He started up, but what had started as a trail had been washed out by the fall rains. Remone had to pull himself up over slippery moss-covered rocks without any secure footing. He continued climbing using the tree roots he could grip to pull himself up. After hours of struggling, he reached the summit of the ridge where he could see clearly in all directions. But his strength was spent. He looked but could see no water and sat down to rest.

The process of humbling Remone and making him into something pliable that the Great Mystery could use had begun. Remone was not religious. His god had no place in his life. Like most men, he grew more religious when he found himself in a time of need. Dying of thirst on top of the mountain ridge made him begin to pray in earnest.

Lord, save me from this heat. If you will just spare my life, I will live differently from this day on. Just let one drop of water fall and wet my tongue. His pleas resembled those of a contestant on the *Let's Make a Deal* show.

Then in the distance, he saw a dark cumulus cloud gathering on the horizon and moving in his direction. In a crack of lightning, he heard the cloud say, "Remone, I come to quench your thirst and save you!"

But the Great Spirit made the sun move out from behind the darkness and admonished the cloud, saying, "No, Remone must suffer to purify himself. He must learn his God's name!" Immediately, the sun turned the cloud into a wisp of vapor.

Farther along the mountainside, Remone crawled, struggling to stand but he was too weak and thirsty. He pulled himself through the brush and bramble, over rocks and boulders until he could see down into the valley below. From the edge of the cliff, he spied a small creek many feet beneath him. But he saw no clear trail to begin a descent. He worked himself into a crevasse and slid down on his backbone until he could go no farther.

He could see the creek more clearly now. There was water rippling over the stones, and there were green shade trees that could provide a needed respite from the sun. He tried to make his way along the cliff with his back against the rock as he felt with his feet for firm ground. He grabbed a vine as he readjusted his foothold, but it could not support his weight. Remone slipped as the vine tore out of the soil.

"Yaaaaahhh!" yelled the lost White man as he bounced down the mountainside, narrowly missing the sharp jagged rocks below as he tumbled. Only the briars and underbrush slowed his fall. The thorns tore his face and hands as he reached out for something to grab onto. Nothing broke his fall until he hit the level ground of the creek bank.

Trying to get back up, he found no energy left in his body and, with a groan, collapsed.

He awoke and crawled to the creek, stuck his head under the water, and drank his fill. Remone sighed and rubbed the large bump on his head. *I'm okay*, thought Remone, *just some painful bruises and scrapes, no broken bones.* He tore loose some grass to chew on as he contemplated his brush with death.

The sun was sinking as a cool breeze began to blow in from the west. A hawk circled overhead, cawing out her song as she hunted for dinner to take back to her nest on the mountain ridge. Remone felt a peace and oneness with the planet, but a sound broke him away from his reverie.

"Remone," a voice called softly on the wind.

Remone heard his name but thought it to be his imagination. He saw a large turtle that had crawled onto the bank and was munching on a brightly colored mushroom. Remone glanced away and felt the wind on his skin.

Again, he heard his name, "Remone," and gasped as the voice seemed to be coming from the turtle. He watched the turtle closely and rubbed the knot on his head.

Again, he heard his name as the turtle's mouth moved, "Remone."

"So what's this?" said Remone. "A talking turtle?"

"My name is Many Faces," said the turtle. "I am much older than you, Remone. I may be moving slowly, but my mind is moving much faster."

"My mind may be moving slower because of the blow to my head. I don't believe I am listening to a talking turtle."

"Why do you search outside for your vision when the answer is within you?"

"I search outside myself because that is where my vision must take place."

"There are those things to explore outside yourself, in outer space, and there are those things to explore inside yourself, in your inner space. In this space, you will find the seed that will sprout into something much bigger from which your spirit can grow. You will find that while still an individual, you are part of an inseparable oneness with the Great Spirit and all he has created."

Spellbound by the turtle's soothing voice, Remone breathed deeply as he listened to the turtle and the melody of the creek as the water trickled over the pebbles.

"I have been sent here to help you. When I was human, I was a seeker. I journeyed the earth looking for answers. Now I continue the journey of learning, only with much smaller steps. Remember, be persistent and you will find your answers."

All at once, there was a rustling, and the door to the sweat lodge was flung open. Pinchot and the shaman helped Remone to his feet and put a buffalo hide over his body to cover his nakedness.

Remone realized he was still in the sweat lodge and had been the whole time. The wilderness he had retreated to was inside his own mind. The vision he had was the result of four days of fasting and sweating himself to a different place he had never been before. Call it just a dream or a vision. It did not matter. Remone had grown from it. He had received a lesson, and his soul had been widened in ways that he did not yet understand.

Remone sat down by the fire. One of the braves handed him a cup of soup while he gathered his senses.

"You have had vision?" the shaman asked.

"I...I don't know," Remone stuttered.

"I know for you. I have seen your vision, the talking turtle. Many times Many Faces has come to me seeking counsel. Your dream has much magic. It is big medicine!"

"Yeah, but a talking turtle? I was expecting a bear, a mountain lion, or maybe even an eagle," Remone said with disappointment.

The shaman became angry. "The vision picks you! You do not pick your vision! Look to the sign of the turtle, Remone. He is persistent and the persistent fool grows wise by it!"

5

T HE DAY WAS A CLOUDY one and threatened rain as Pinchot and Remone hunted the woods around the village. They followed the river down along its banks where the deer came to drink and eat the bark off the trees.

"Let us hurry and get dinner before we get wet," Pinchot said as they tried to avoid stepping on any sticks that would give their prey warning.

"Here I will show you how to call the deer," said Pinchot. "This is the cry of the deer." Pinchot took a folded leaf and placed it between his lips and blew on it forcefully.

Remone thought, *It sounds a little like a kazoo.*

But it worked, as Pinchot heard the cracking sound of a branch in the thicket and motioned for Remone to stop. "Stay here and I will try to flush the deer in your direction. Have your arrow ready." With the agility of a cat, Pinchot quickly and silently disappeared.

Remone placed an arrow on his bowstring and stooped behind a bush where he had a view of the clump of trees Pinchot had gone into. But the hunter tired of waiting, and his concentration drifted. He imagined himself as the center of the tribe's attention. In his daydream, he brought back two large deer, already dressed by himself. He carried them one over each shoulder, their heads resting on his manly chest, tongues hanging out of their open mouths. He would drop them at Chief Slow Bull's feet where the village enjoyed its communal fire. The chief would rise in respect of the prize, and Amber Moon would clasp her hands to her chest as she admired the great hunter Remone.

Without warning, the deer burst out of the thicket and into the clearing, running directly toward Remone. He saw the antlers, and it looked to be a six-pointer. But Remone was not ready, and the deer was at a full run. The buck began to zigzag as he raced for his life, and Remone released his arrow, but it flew behind the accelerating deer. The stag leaped over a fallen tree and was gone.

An upset Pinchot was not far behind the deer. "How did you miss? That was an easy shot," he said as he ran up to where Remone stood.

Remone had no answer, just a stupid blank expression. His fantasy of himself as the great hunter was shattered. Silence accompanied the pair as they traveled farther into the woods. Remone sulked at the sting of Pinchot's criticism of his marksmanship with the bow.

To Remone, it seemed that Pinchot bore the pressure of feeding the tribe on his shoulders alone. "Why do you take on the responsibility of feeding the tribe? Is it to win the approval of Chief Slow Bull and the tribe's elders?"

An irritated Pinchot sat down on a fallen tree and motioned for Remone to do the same. "In this, you are in error, Remone. Let me tell you of what a much younger Pinchot saw as a young man. While hunting, I came upon an injured fox who had lost one of his legs. I wondered how he had survived without being able to hunt for himself. I watched as a mountain lion approached, carrying a piece of meat in his mouth. 'Here, the Great Spirit has sent me to care for you,' the mountain lion said as he sat down in front of the fox, ate his fill, and left the rest of the meat for the fox.

"I came back the next day to see what would happen. On this day, a large hawk flew down to the ground carrying a fish in its mouth. 'Here this is for you,' the bird said, dropping the fish at the fox's feet and flying away.

"I marveled at the Great Mystery and how he cared for all his creation that he should watch over a fox in the wild. I pondered his greatness and said to myself, I, too, shall put my full trust in him. He will provide me with all I need. So I camped in the wilderness and prayed to the Great Spirit and waited and waited. For many days, I did no hunting, for I knew the Great Mystery would provide for me. All I had to do was believe. Soon I was weak, for I had only water to drink with nothing to eat. Then I heard the voice of the Great Spirit,

'Oh, you, foolish one, who are on the wrong path. Open your eyes to the truth! Stop imitating the disabled and follow the example of the mountain lion and hawk.'

"I realized I was not in need and what I must do was take action. Instead of waiting to be saved by the Great Spirit, I needed to act on his behalf. To help those who were in need and suffered from injuries. That should be my mission."

"So you learned your role was in doing, not waiting for the Great Spirit to do it for you?" asked Remone.

"Yes, this was a turning point in my young life. This event led me to be the hunter that I am today. It lies heavily on my heart to be the one to provide food for the tribe and especially for those who are unable to do it for themselves."

"So that is why you prepare food and take it to the old widow, Wakiya."

"Yes, many times I have had to hold her head up to feed her so she will not choke on the food as I serve it to her."

"And I know you also go to Alowan's teepee."

"Yes, Alowan fell from his horse in the buffalo hunt. He was trampled by the bulls, and his legs have never been the same. You may have seen him on his crutches making his way slowly through the village and warming himself at the tribe's fire. He has been unable to hunt since his accident, but as the moons pass, he leaves his teepee less. That is why I take him food. That is why I am here. This is what the Great Spirit asks me to do."

"And this all goes back to your days as a young brave?"

"Yes, I try to act on the lessons this life has taught me. We all must learn to serve the Great Mystery with humility. I see those who suffer, and it troubles me. We must all strive to control our pride and give what we have, to share."

As they sat talking, Remone looked up to see a deer standing perfectly still above them on the hill. He pointed to the deer and motioned for Pinchot to take the shot.

"No, this one is yours, Remone. Just don't miss," Pinchot said with a smile.

6

A NEWBORN WAS CONSIDERED SACRED TO the Sioux, having arrived from the spiritual realm. The Sioux believed that before a baby was born into this world, the child looked upon all the people and chose their mother and father. These beliefs were the reason the tribe put so much effort into the raising of each infant. Everyone in the village played a role in looking after the children. The women raised the young maidens in the way they should grow, teaching them how to prepare food and decorate clothes. The men raised the boys, teaching them the way of the hunt. But the most important lesson that was taught was the spiritual nature of life.

White children might attend a classroom of brick or wood. The young braves used the great outdoors for their classroom. Instead of textbooks, they gathered around the shaman to learn from him. This day, the shaman, along with Pinchot and Remone, had taken a group of boys into the woods where they sat on the ground, enjoying the sun as it warmed them.

The shaman picked up an acorn off the ground and stood up, holding it up to the sun and pondering its size. "As the tiny acorn grows into a mighty tree, so it is with soul growth. From the smallest seed planted deep within your soul, a human being can grow into a great leader, a light unto his people."

"Which is most important—knowledge or wisdom? What say you, Pinchot?" the shaman asked his most reliable elder of the tribe.

"The Whites know enough to create a rifle, but they do not have enough wisdom to know when to use it. He shoots animals for sport and not for need. He may find himself without later because of his lack of judgment."

The young males listened intently, wide-eyed, as they tried to absorb the lesson.

"Remember, when one prays to the Great Spirit, he must both talk and listen to hear the answer. Train yourself to listen!" said the shaman. "Wakan Tanka should receive thanks for everything on this earth. Gratitude unlocks the fullness of life. The deeper our gratitude, the more we receive out of life, for it has not gone unnoticed."

"The brave must look to what he feeds himself upon and not drink from the creek of bitter waters. Know that you will be tempted to stray from the path in the pursuits of the flesh, stomach, and other false glories," the shaman said as he continued his lesson.

"It is man's own mind, not another's, that lures him to evil ways," added Pinchot.

Later, when they had left the students, Remone asked the shaman, "Why do you concern yourself with the path of the braves so much when they are so young?"

"It is hard to change the flight of the arrow once it has left the bow," the shaman answered as he continued walking to Chief Slow Bull's teepee.

7

CLIMBING UP THE MOUNTAIN WAS difficult in the darkness, but the display in the skies made the trip worth it. The shaman had a reason for picking this place on this night. A clear night with no moon made the view of the stars amazing. From the bluff, one could see the full horizon unobstructed by trees.

The maps that could be found in the stars was an important part of the braves' learning the ways of the hunt. Pointing out a single star was not an easy way to navigate the sky, so like most civilizations, the Sioux chose patterns of stars to make it easier to give directions. The tales they told of their heroes in the sky made it easier to remember the different star clusters.

Remone gathered wood as Pinchot stoked the fire.

"Who can see the North Star, the Hunter's Star?" the shaman asked.

One of the oldest boys, Tusca, said, "There it is," as he pointed in its direction.

"Yes, very good. It does not move like the other stars in the sky. The sky spins around it, giving you a stable point of direction. Remember this when you are hunting and get lost and are afraid of freezing to death without a teepee and nothing but wet wood to burn. Know it to be a part of the constellation of the Thunderbird Wakinyan, who rules the winter nights. See the stars that make up his right wing," said the shaman, pointing and tracing his staff across the sky, "and his left wing. See his talons below?"

Sitting back down at the fire, the shaman began a tale from which all the braves could gain insight and maybe remember how to locate crucial directions in the night sky. "Listen to the story of Tulumtec, a Sioux brave not much older than yourselves.

"The winter had started to warm into spring, and the time had come for a young brave, Tulumtec, who had reached manhood, to begin his vision quest. He gathered his bow, arrows, and blankets into a pack. The journey required one to take no food. The elders of the tribe gathered to see him off. The old shaman, Shanshurack, presented him with a talisman to protect him on his quest. He bid him a safe journey, and Tulumtec set off down the trail full of excitement with the energy of a young man on a great adventure, sure of his skills as a hunter.

"He sang an old Sioux hunting song, 'Hiya-ho down the trail I go, looking for the buffalo grove,' as he cheerfully made his way up the mountain. He reached the top and, looking down, saw a deer scouring the tree branches for something to eat. He tried to sneak up on the doe, but a snapping branch announced his approach. He let his arrow fly from some distance, missing the deer. 'Not today, Tulumtec, for I am a mother deer and have babies to feed,' she said, leaping away.

"He ran after the deer for a short distance until he lost her in the thicket. Turning around, he went back to look for the trail but found he had lost his way from the path that the elders had urged him to stay on.

"The early spring rains descended upon him and reminded him that winter was not yet entirely over. Cold came creeping as he lay down against a tree in his soaked blanket and sat, shivering until the sun slowly came back out.

"Tulumtec searched the woods for something to eat, but none of the spring plants had emerged yet from the long winter snows. He saw an occasional squirrel, but then a bird flew to within a short distance of Tulumtec. While the pheasant pecked the ground, looking for seeds, he tried to sneak up on it. He drew back on his bow, but it took flight before he could take good aim. His arrow flew, but it fell short of hitting the quail. 'You'll have to be a better shot than that, Tulumtec, if you want to eat me,' the bird sang out as he flew away.

"Tulumtec slept in the open with no fire to warm his wet body. A long night passed by slowly. His thoughts drifted back to his upraising as an orphan by the Shaman Shanshurack. His mother had died while birthing him, and his father was killed in a skirmish with the Crows. The shaman as his teacher had taught him many of the skills needed to lead the tribe and to care for their health by knowing the special herbs of the woods. He learned how to call out the Great Spirit's name and ask him questions. He learned that he was not the center of the universe but was part of something much greater.

"In the morning, he began another day in search of the nourishment that would keep him alive. He saw deer tracks in the mud and started breathing faster as he excitedly charged up the trail, following the tracks. When he reached the crest of the hill, he dropped his hands to his knees and wheezed as he watched a pair of deer, a doe, and a buck disappearing into the trees.

"Peeling back the bark of one of the maple trees, Tulumtec tried chewing the bark and fought to keep down the only food he had found while he looked for something better. After searching until dusk, he lifted a rock and found little white grubs slithering about on their thousands of little legs. He was so hungry he lowered himself to eating one. Tulumtec lifted it to his mouth and bit it in half. He scrunched his face in disgust. It tasted horrible. He swallowed the rest whole so he wouldn't have to taste any more.

"He awoke cold, hungry, and lost in the wilderness after another night of sleeping in the cold. He came upon a creek and thought he would try fishing. He worked a piece of bone into a hook and used his bowstring as a line.

"After a while of throwing out his hook, Tulumtec struggled to remain conscious and was about to give up when a large trout came to the surface and said, 'Tulumtec, I will let you catch me if you promise to eat me.' 'You would do this for me? For I am sore with hunger?' 'I will do this because I know I will live inside you and become a part of you, just as the water I drink and breathe becomes a part of me. Where is one separate from the other? In this way, we live forever.'

"Feeling a tug on his line, Tulumtec pulled the fish from the water and started a fire. He roasted the trout on a spit he made from a sapling that was still green and wouldn't burn in the fire.

"Nourished with his meal, he continued on his journey looking for a place to sleep, as it was cold and looked like it might rain. A cave he saw in the base of a cliff looked like a good place to pass the night. He gathered some firewood and stepped up into the cave. With a piece of kindling, he started a fire and warmed the cave. But as light from the fire fell on the walls of the cave, Tulumtec saw that he was not alone. A large brown grizzly bear had also chosen this cave as his home for the winter.

"The bear growled, awakening from his slumbers, 'What are you doing here? I had another month to sleep.' 'I am sorry to have disturbed your rest,' Tulumtec said to the bear. 'Let me continue on my journey and I will bother you no more, for I am on a religious quest to find out how to be one with Wakan Tanka and receive my vision. I will soon know what animal spirit I can gain my strength from.'

"The bear was groggy and moved slowly as he swung at the young brave. Tulumtec dodged the claw of the sleepy bear and ran out of the cave as fast as he could, leaving his blankets and his bow and arrows behind. 'Come back,' the angry bear cried. 'I can make you one with the universe once I eat you!' Tulumtec fled with only his knife, which he carried in a sheath around his waist. He suffered much, lost in the snow with no shelter and little hope. What mistake did Tulumtec make?"

The young braves answered, "He strayed from the path and lost his way."

"The message of this story is clear," Pinchot said. "Do not let the excitement of the hunt cloud your judgment. Do not lose sight of the path."

"Well said, Pinchot, for without restraint one will never grow old enough to have experience," the shaman responded.

"As he lay shivering in the in the woods in great despair," the shaman continued, "Tulumtec did the only thing he could do. He prayed to the Great One, knowing the Great Spirit hears all prayers. Hearing the prayer, the Great Mystery sent the Thunderbird Wakinyan to be Tulumtec's animal guide. He carried maize covered in honey in his talons. This magical food gave Tulumtec the strength to continue.

"The Thunderbird took Tulumtec flying high into the sky on his back and showed him many things and told him even more. Tulumtec's innocent eyes were opened further than those of men twice his age. He saw far into the future in visions that revealed to him the end of the human race at the White man's own hand.

"Wakinyan the Great Thunderbird explained all to Tulumtec, 'You have been chosen to be a great shaman for the Sioux people. You will see more traveling through time to learn and lead your people. Prophesize the folly of the White man as they work only to destroy all, even the very earth upon which they walk.'

"'What fools would destroy that upon which they walk?' asked Tulumtec. 'Only the White man as soon as he can,' answered the Thunderbird, 'for he has been blinded in his pursuit of power.' 'I give you the gift of my animal sign,' said the Thunderbird, 'but it is a heavy gift, as you will see further than other men into the future and into men's hearts. Not always a blessing and sometimes a curse, for you will have the weight of a prophet upon your shoulders. The Whites will destroy the earth because of their insatiable greed, but all will be returned to the Sioux in time. Even the buffalo will return to cover the plains in their great number again as in the earlier days, when the Great Mystery ordains it and Mother Earth has been purified of the Whites.'

"Returning to the village, Tulumtec looked different, for his hair had turned white as snow. Only the old Shaman Shanshurack recognized him. 'It is Tulumtec returned from a great journey—see here is the talisman I gave him!'

"The old shaman could see from Tulumtec's glowing silver-blue aura that he had been greatly changed outwardly and inside as well. Taking him under his wing, Shanshurack continued to teach Tulumtec the shaman's way of Sioux's magic and healing.

"Anointing him to be his successor, the old Shaman Shanshurack spoke to his people, 'I have chosen Tulumtec to be the spiritual leader in my stead, for his heart and mine are on the same path that the Great Spirit has chosen for both of us. His animal totem is the

Thunderbird, and he has given him the power of sight. He sees inside himself and others. I am old and fading in the sunset. He is young yet wiser than his years. He will guide you.'

"For many years, Tulumtec led the tribe. The legacy of the shaman's role as spiritual leader and physician to the tribe continued from generation to generation. The Sioux grew into the greatest of all the Plains Indians with his guidance.

"Many years later, while sitting on a mountaintop, Tulumtec heard a crack of thunder and then the voice of an old friend, saying, 'Time to go.' It was the Great Thunderbird Wakinyan. 'Wakan Tanka has claimed you as his own and has sent me to take you to your reward.'

"Tulumtec climbed onto the Thunderbird's back, and they flew up through the sky higher than ever before. Up to the highest heights, past the moon, to the outskirts of infinity and beyond until they were one with the stars assuming their place in the constellations.

"And there just above the constellation of the Thunderbird Wakinyan is the figure of Tulumtec in the winter sky," the shaman said as he pointed with his staff.

8

"REMONE HAS GROWN IN THE Sioux way," said the shaman. "It is time to teach him of the medicine wheel. The wheel is one of our most sacred sites. Built by our ancestors, it honors the four winds."

"Yes, I want to see the wheel for myself," Remone said. "Pinchot has told me it sits on sacred ground, where we can see a great distance."

Together the three set out on the long hike up to the top of the mountain. The shaman pushed himself along with his staff while Pinchot and Remone stopped to take in the beauty of each vista they came to. This gave time for the older shaman to keep up with them.

"Early spring is a beautiful time. Mother Earth binds us all together spiritually," the shaman said as he sat down on a fallen tree and pulled out his water bag to drink from. "Did you see the eagle's nest on the side of the cliff?" The shaman pointed with his staff to where the pine tree had pushed its way through the rock, giving it a twisted bonsai look. A large nest sat perched on top of the branches.

"The mother eagle must be out hunting for food," Pinchot said as he shaded his eyes with his hand. "From here you can see the headwaters of the Cheyenne River that runs through our village."

The shaman took out his pipe as the trio rested in the sunlight. Snow still lay in patches on the ground under the shade of the trees.

Remone yawned. "The sun feels good. I am ready for spring."

"Soon the fishing will be good." Pinchot smiled. "We must go bow fishing. It has been too cold."

"Look, the eagle," the shaman said in a whisper as he pointed up in the sky.

"Let's see if she returns to the nest," said Remone as he stood to see better.

Above all the cliffs and rock outbreaks, the eagle soared gracefully in the light of the sun. She did not have to flap her wings, only glide on the updrafts of air pushing her higher.

All three sat for a moment, in awe of the beauty of the day. Pinchot waved to get Remone's attention and pointed at the shaman, whose eyes were closed as he snored slightly. Their laughter stirred the shaman from his rest.

"We need to get moving, or we will not have any daylight," the shaman said as stood up with his staff, ready to continue their ascent.

The three trudged on, back to the trail and continuing their journey to the Wheel. When they reached the summit, the shaman said, "Look, we are here." He pointed at the panoramic view of the mountains in the distance and the valley far below. The terrain at the wheel leveled out, but the surrounding rock structure encircling the area gave it a bowl-like shape. It looked like an arena to Remone. On the northern side of the structure was a rock that rose just high enough for one to stand and address the tribe. To Remone, it looked like a pulpit carved out of rock.

As they got closer, he could see the wheel that had been built there with the four main spokes splitting the wheel equally. The wheel represented the four winds and the four seasons that blew through the Sioux's lives. The wheel itself showed their belief that life was lived in cycles, the perfect circle of life. Everything that happened had happened before and would happen again.

"No cathedral in Europe holds as much beauty as this place," said Remone with a sigh.

"What is a cathedral?" asked Pinchot.

"A large building where we worship our God."

"Why would one worship the Great One inside a house?"

"I don't know after seeing this place. I can see why the Sioux look at it with such reverence."

Remone thought about how some people obsessed about their church building, seeking to make it more and more ornate until it becomes just another false idol instead of a place in which to seek God. The church building itself became a deterrent to finding God as much as any golden calf forged in the wilderness.

I would probably have wanted to put a bunch of condos on this site if I was still in real estate. Now he saw why the Indians looked at the White man with such disdain. The termite people, as they referred to them, destroyed everything they touched because of their greed. And this is what the White man called progress.

The shaman reached into his pouch and pulled out a piece of sage. He untied it and used his flint to light the dried end. As it caught fire, he blew it out, letting it smolder. The smoke traveled on the wind. The shaman rose to his feet and shook the sweet smoke first to the east, chanting, "To the east and the rising sun, we celebrate this day we have been given. To the south where all life comes from, we welcome your warm and pleasant winds. To the west and the setting sun, we thank you for the rains you bring. And to the north, bringing the cleansing cold, may we all face your winds head-on into the storm like our buffalo brothers, learning patience and endurance. We thank our ancestors for all they have done to give us life and wisdom."

The shaman placed the remaining sage on the ground and sat down cross-legged beside Remone.

"What good does it do to burn the sage?" Remone asked the shaman.

"It honors our ancestors who dwell in the land of spirits, who gave life to us. We the living must show respect for those who came before."

"How do the dead even know that you do this for them?"

"Because the past is still alive," the shaman answered. "What happened in the past remains a vital and active invisible presence in the life of our people today."

"Like building one step on another?" said Remone. "Like if I want to practice law or medicine, I have to get a degree, and that determines what I can do in the future?"

"No, that is not the same thing," the shaman said in the tired voice of one whose patience was spent. "The knowledge that you acquire affects what you can do today, but this is different. You are thinking like a White man. I have felt my grandfather's presence in my life because one way he has chosen to speak to me is through my dreams."

"Do you really think it is your grandfather and not just a dream you are having about him?"

"He has come to me looking just like he did when he passed onto the spirit world. His words to me were harsh. He did not approve of my actions and wanted me to change my path. 'Why did you accept the White man Remone into the tribe?' Grandfather asked me. 'He is White and will never understand our way. You waste your breath and wisdom.' He is angry at me, so I burn sage to honor his memory and to calm his restless spirit."

Remone laughed uneasily at what he hoped was said in jest.

"Another time my grandfather came to me and asked me to forgive a rival in the tribe." The shaman looked away as he was reliving the moment. The shaman's face grew more serious and tense as Remone watched and listened. "This is one who had spoken poorly of me and my medicine. In my anger, I thought, *He does not think my medicine works? I will show him how well it works.* But I was younger then and foolish."

"But what happened?" asked Remone.

"I am ashamed to say that I called upon the spirits to make the man sick even close to death. On a moonless night, I took the blood of a dead skunk and crept into his teepee where he lay sleeping and marked his forehead in a cross of blood, leaving the dead skunk's remains at his door. I chanted under my breath quietly the curse I was casting. Circling his teepee four times, I slinked back to my teepee to an unsettling sleepless night.

"In a matter of days, it had begun. The brave was seen wobbling through the village as he vomited blood. He was no longer able to hunt, and after a week, he had lost weight and was unable to rise from his bed. At first, I relished my power and felt justified in what I had done. Then my grandfather, who had also been a shaman, came to me in a dream. 'You have been given your gift to lead and help your people. You now make me regret our bloodline. Turn from this path and ask the Great Spirit to forgive your injustice.'"

"What did you do?"

Pinchot put his finger to his lips, signaling Remone to be silent while the shaman continued.

"I went into the wilderness and prayed for forgiveness for what I had done. I fasted and practiced blood sacrifice on my body as penance. The voice of Wakan Tanka came to me and clearly said, 'In order to be forgiven, you must forgive.' Immediately, I left the woods, returned to the village, and sought out the brave I had wronged. He lay in his teepee, still sick. First, I ministered to him in his weakened state, burning sage in and around his teepee to purify it. I took him special waters from the Wasca Springs. Then I prayed over him as I held his weakened head so he could drink the waters and keep down the first nourishment he had in over a week.

"As he recovered, he expressed remorse. 'Here I told lies about you to cast doubt on your ability as a healer, and yet you have healed me. How can I face the tribe?' 'I will tell you how,' I said. 'For I have done you a greater injustice. I knew that you had talked unjustly about me, and in my anger, I caused your illness. It is I who must seek forgiveness from you.'

"The two of us embraced and I left his tepee," said the shaman, "feeling like two weights had been removed. My anger was extinguished like a fire put out by a hard rain, and my guilt was gone. I had been forgiven by him, whom I had wronged, and by the Great Spirit."

9

Having spent his whole life
with a heavy yoke on his back,
he never noticed the extra weight
until they removed it.

WITH THE ARRIVAL OF THE horse, the Indian hunter was able to travel farther and faster in pursuit of his primary food source, the buffalo. The Plains Indians quickly became the most skilled horsemen the world had ever seen, able to ride low enough to shield themselves with the horse's flanks while shooting over the horse's neck, all without the use of a saddle. Skill with the horse was as important a part of the brave's education as the use of the bow and arrow. Both skills served them well on the hunt when riding in the middle of a thundering herd of buffalo.

"Hold the bridle tighter," Pinchot shouted as Remone, dug his fingers into the horse's mane while trying to keep pace with his mentor.

"It's hard to stay balanced!" cried Remone as he slid to the ground and, with a great acrobatic move, found himself running beside the horse instead of falling facedown into the dirt.

Pinchot frowned as he rode back to Remone. "Pull the bridle tighter and take the horse down the path you choose."

With great effort, Remone threw himself back onto the horse. The horse responded by rearing up and kicking his front feet into the air. "I think my horse has chosen his own path!"

Pinchot laughed as Remone's horse, Travelor, took off galloping at full speed through the briers, trying to dismount his rider.

Branches whipped his face as Remone tried to shield himself with one hand and tighten his grip on the halter with the other. Pinchot slowly followed his adopted brother at a distance.

Time passed before Remone emerged from the other side of the woods still mounted, his face scratched and bleeding from the branches and briers. But he was in control of his horse. Remone had let him run himself out. Now the horse respected Remone after having challenged him and lost.

"Remone has learned to ride like Sioux today!" said an excited Pinchot as he brought his horse to a stop to get a good look at Remone's face. "Horse teach you a lesson not easy to forget!"

Smiling back at Pinchot but feeling as if he had been split in half from the buttocks up, Remone said, "I might want to go lay in the Wasco Hot Springs tonight."

Laughing, Pinchot turned his horse back to the trail, and they started up the ridge. Pinchot wanted to take Remone to Eagle's Nest on their way back to the valley. The more elevation they gained, the better the view. The afternoon turned to early evening as they stopped to watch eagles flying to the rocky crest to feed their young with the fish they had caught in the river below.

"See how the Great Spirit lights the world for us! So that we who are blind might see his glory!" Pinchot said as they ascended the trail.

Remone felt a feeling of liberation he had never experienced before. The setting sun shone down on the mountain ridge as they rode on. The distant horizon was painted in a red glow. Miles away, they could see the herd of buffalo in the valley making their way through Buffalo Pass, looking for greener pastures. Remone was filled with euphoria, as if a great weight had been lifted from his back. *The responsibilities that weighed me down seem so pointless now. I will never go back to what I knew. I am so happy to be here. This is the most I have ever enjoyed my life.*

"Who will be the first back to the camp?" shouted Pinchot as he kicked his horse into a gallop.

Remone snapped out of his daydream and urged his mount on, galloping after Pinchot.

A saddle-sore Remone limped from the horse line, joining Pinchot, the shaman, and Chief Slow Bull around the communal fire.

"So the little fish you pulled from the river has ridden horse-back?" Slow Bull asked.

"My student has learned much of horse riding today?" Pinchot answered.

"Who was his teacher?'

"From a stallion named Travelor. He has learned much."

Assuming a humble position before Chief Slow Bull, Remone silently listened to him and the elders of the tribe. The chief's intim-idating manner made Remone uncomfortable. He felt his gaze when he locked it on him, and it made him feel small, but mostly the chief made a point to not acknowledge Remone at all. He never talked directly to him, just about him to other members of the tribe as if he was not there. Remone knew it was because he had not gained the chief's respect or earned his trust.

"What of our horses and the Crow who crowd our hunting grounds?" the chief asked the elders.

Meeting around the fire, they discussed many things—from the diminishing herds of buffalo to planning the next raid on the Crow tribe whose camp was nearby. Slow Bull agreed Pinchot should lead the attack on the Crow.

"I will test the mettle of the White and take him to face the Crow," Pinchot said.

"What of the White?" Slow Bull asked. "Has he learned any skills? What would make him worthy of going on the raid?"

"It is time for the trials of the White known as Remone to begin. Only the Great Mystery can decide whether he will survive to become Sioux," Pinchot said, presenting his case calmly to the chief.

"Yes, it is time to for us to consider what will take him from white soft papoose to man!" said the shaman.

"Giving blood to Wakan Tanka," answered Pinchot.

"Seeing the auras," said the shaman.

"And coming to face his worst nightmare," added Chief Slow Bull.

All of this was discussed openly in front of Remone, but he did not comprehend how any of it would play a part in his destiny to become a Sioux brave. Slow Bull had not accepted Remone's presence but did respect the opinions of Pinchot and the shaman, both highly respected in the tribe. They were the proponents of Remone's advancement in the Sioux way.

The half-moon had started to set on the horizon when Pinchot, Remone, and the other braves stole their way into the Crow village. Pinchot had picked the time closest to dawn when the Crows slept, and the night was blackest.

In the cover of darkness, they broke down the makeshift fence and with a howl let the Crow know their village was violated. The Crow lookout was the first upon the Sioux, but it was too late. Running up brandishing the blunt end of his spear, Remone rendered him unconscious with a blow to the head before he could hurl his weapon. Pinchot jumped astride one of the biggest horses and started herding the rest, screeching his war cry to get the horses moving and to intimidate the Crows as they stumbled from their teepees.

Remone jumped on a white mustang and set his fingers deep in the pony's mane to secure his grip as he galloped. The excitement was contagious as he yelled at the horses, moving them forward into the night. Pinchot smiled at him, laughing as they rode through the snow, putting as much distance as they could between them and the Crow village.

The sunrise lit the valley as they rode down the river path to their village. Awake with excitement, the village turned out to greet the braves as they returned with their bounty of horses.

"Remone has picked a fine pony!" Pinchot shouted loud enough for all to hear.

Remone, beaming with excitement, jumped from the mustang, slapping Pinchot on the back as he exclaimed, "A great prize for the tribe!"

They herded all the horses and ponies and tied them to their horse line. The tribe greeted them with calls of congratulations. The women brought food to the braves. As they celebrated, Pinchot asked Remone, "What name will your pony go by?"

"Am I worthy of such a gift?"

"The pony chose you from among all the other braves."

"I will treasure this gift and name him Little Wing, as he is small but swift in his flight."

The Crows could easily have followed the horse prints in the snow but without their horses would have been at a disadvantage. Still, the Sioux put extra braves on watch to guard against any retribution on the part of the Crow. The whole tribe praised the successful raid except for Black Wolf, who was furious after learning of the gift of the pony to Remone.

10

"TUSCA, WHAT ANIMAL LEFT THIS track?" asked Pinchot as he crouched down on one knee.

Tusca bent down to look at the track. "It looks like a rabbit track to me."

"Here, Chatan, you look at it and tell me what you think." Pinchot waved for all the young braves to move in closer and squatted down to try to identify the tracks.

"I think it may be a squirrel track," said Chatan with some hesitation.

"Good guess, both of you, but this looks to me like an opossum track. Not the best food, unless you were very hungry. Knowing the tracks will help keep you from wasting your time hunting down animals you do not have a taste for."

Pinchot, the shaman, and Remone had taken a group of boys away from the village, where their lessons for living in the wilderness could be practiced. They would rely on themselves for their meals. Being hungry made them appreciate their school in the woods even more.

"Look at this track here," said Remone as he stood away from the group and pointed to the ground. "What does it look like?"

The group moved over to where Remone had knelt to look at the track closer.

Pinchot picked the brave standing closest to the track. "What do you think, Chippewa?"

Chippewa got down to look at the shape left in the dirt. "It looks to me like it might have been left by a cat."

"That would be good to know," said Pinchot. "Not only something that you could not eat but also something that could kill you. Does anyone else want to guess what animal these tracks belong to?"

The young braves stood back and waited for Pinchot's expertise to answer for them.

"This would be good food," Pinchot said. "These look like coyote tracks. Let us see if we can pick up this trail."

Later that day, they had not found any coyote, only three squirrels and one rabbit.

"Remone and I are heading back to the camp to start cooking these," Pinchot said as he picked the squirrels off Tusca's shoulder. "You need to stay and find us something else to eat."

The braves followed the aroma of squirrel stew back to the camp.

"Our hunters have returned!" Pinchot said as the braves stepped into the clearing.

"But do they have dinner for us?" asked the shaman.

"Two more rabbits and a quail," Chippewa said as he held up the two rabbits.

"Fine rabbits. Who shot the quail?" Pinchot asked the braves.

"It was my arrow who found the quail!" said Chippewa as he presented it to Pinchot and the shaman.

"We will have to remember that Chippewa is a very good shot with the bow," the shaman said, flattering the young brave.

After they had filled themselves with squirrel and rabbit stew, the shaman and Pinchot let the braves lead the discussion and answer their questions as best they could.

"How will I find the animal who will aid me through my life?" Chenoa asked.

"You will not find your animal totem. It will find you. The Great Spirit knows your heart and what friend he needs to send to your aid," the shaman said as he filled his pipe.

"There is one among you named for the animal from which he draws his strength," Pinchot said as he turned to Chatan. "How did you receive help from your animal friend, Chatan?"

"My name from the womb had been Ayita. But I remember well the time I went hunting as a young boy. I ignored my father's advice to stay close to the village and wandered farther into the woods than I should have. It began to storm, so I took cover in a cave, but when the rain stopped, I could not find my way back to the village. I could not see the sun through the clouds and could not tell east from west. Darkness fell and I could see no stars to point my way back home," said Chatan as he choked with emotion remembering his ordeal.

"It is hard even for a skilled brave to read the map in the sky when there is no sun or stars to see," Pinchot said as he empathized with Chatan. "What did you do?"

"I went back to the cave and stayed the night, cold and hungry. I prayed to Wakan Tanka, asking him to show me the way back. I fell asleep. Morning came and still there was no sun, only clouds and no answer from the Great Mystery!"

"The answer does not always come easily or in the way we expect when we ask our prayer," said the shaman. "Keeping one's head clear and ears open helps for us to hear the Great Spirit's reply."

"The woods were completely still with no breeze blowing," Chatan continued. "All I heard was the cawing of a hawk. Through the fog, I could see him sitting in the top branches of an elm tree. At first, I ignored his call. He is just hungry, I thought, just waiting to glide down on some smaller prey. But then I thought, why would he be hunting in this fog? So I came closer to the tree. Again, he called, but this time, I was listening. 'Ayita, the Great Spirit has sent me to help you. Follow me and I will make you a great hunter, just as I am. You will see from great heights and know where the game is that you seek. Come with me and I will guide you back to the village.'

"The hawk flapped his wings, circled the tree and flew to a pine a short way from where I stood. I quickly ran and stood beneath the tree and cried, 'I follow, lead on!' Soon, I was back with my father. He took me to his chest and then scolded me. 'We have been looking for you! Where have you been?' I told him my story of how the hawk guided me back to the village. And he said my new name was now Chatan, our name for hawk, for most certainly he was my animal totem. And he has always been there for me, ready to assist me in the hunt."

"Very good, Chatan," said the shaman, nodding slowly. "In this way, the Great Mystery knows what is best for each of us as he guides us. He answers our prayers, but often we are not listening or we do not like the answer. Many times, what we pray for is not what we need or may hurt us, so when the answer is no, we think he is not listening."

"Here, have some of my hot tea," Pinchot said to the shaman as he refilled his cup.

"Look to the west. See the constellation of the Great Bear," the shaman said as he pointed with his staff.

"Where?" said Tusca as he came to stand behind the shaman.

"I do not think I see it either," said Chippewa as he, too, came around to stand behind the shaman.

"There, see the bright pair of stars? Those two points are his eyes," the shaman said as he sketched an imaginary line with his staff. "And below that are the smaller stars that make up his face. Then these stars are the chest and these are his flank."

"Oh, I see it now!" Chippewa said. "Is it like the Hunter's Star? Can you use it to find your way?"

"Not as much as the Hunter's Star," answered the shaman. "This constellation crosses the sky and is not visible in the winter. It returns in the spring and stays for the summer when its hibernation is over, just like a bear."

The group sat quietly at the fire, looking up into the sky.

The silence was broken by Tusca, who asked the shaman, "Have you ever seen the Purple Buffalo?"

"No, I have never seen him," said the shaman.

"Then how do you know he exists?" asked Tusca.

"There are many things I cannot see that I know exist. I cannot see him but I believe in the Great Spirit because I see what he has created and have felt his presence in my life."

"But isn't the legend of the Purple Buffalo something more like folklore?" asked Remone at the wrong time. "If no one has seen him?"

"Only one chosen by the Great Mystery to see the Purple Buffalo sees it," said an angry shaman. "There are those who have seen!"

The shaman walked away from the fire and unrolled his bedroll. Pinchot and Remone remained at the fire talking to the braves until the moon sank in the sky and the young braves had gone to sleep.

Pinchot asked Remone, "Why do you anger the shaman? Do you question the way he teaches?"

"No, of course not. He knows more than I."

"Be careful, then, that you do not disrupt his lessons."

With that, Pinchot retired, leaving Remone alone at the fire to ponder what he had said.

11

Paha Sapa, the Black Hills

O F ALL THE EARTH, THE Lakota Sioux loved the Black Hills the most. It was named such because the slopes and peaks were so heavily covered with dark pines, that from the distance the mountains looked black. It looked like an island rising out of the plains. Pure water and abundant game made it a paradise for the Sioux nation.

Pinchot rode his horse, Splitting Cloud, up the trail into the hills. He had chosen this name because the first time he saw his mare, she rode out of a cloud of fog that made it look as if she were splitting it in half. A beautiful and fearless mount, Splitting Cloud was not one to lose her nerve in a fight or when running beside a herd of buffalo. Remone followed Pinchot up the trail on his pony, Little Wing.

"The Great Mystery has favored the Sioux above all other people," Pinchot said to Remone as the pair stopped to look at the view. "Look at what he has given to us. It is up to us, the Sioux, to protect Mother Earth from all who would violate her."

The sun rose with millions of crickets worshipping it as they raised a chorus in homage to the new day. A wave of wind whipped a cloud of mist toward the bluff. Inhaling the deep pine scent of the woods, Remone agreed with Pinchot. "The Sioux have been blessed."

"Would you like me to take you behind Mother Earth's veil? To see behind the shawl that hides her many charms, all this may be revealed to Remone so that she may nurture you on her soft white breasts," Pinchot said as he pointed to the twin peaks in the distance. "You will see what other Whites would *die* to lay their eyes on."

Pinchot had heard that the White man caught a fever when their eyes saw gold. And gold was not difficult to find in the Black Hills. It was everywhere—in the creek beds, in the roots of the pine trees, in quartz veins, and under rocks. Long ago, Pinchot had heard the story that one of the braves from the Rosebud tribe had told.

"I saw it myself," the old brave told them. "Down at the trading post when I was many years younger. We had just taken a bale of beaver pelts to trade with the Whites for horses. White Eagle and I had been hunting for weeks on the river. Many a beaver had we caught in our traps. White Eagle told me the Whites loved the shiny rocks, so he filled a pouch to sell to them.

"They were fair to us in giving us horses for beaver pelts, but as soon as White Eagle showed them the gold, a group of men we had not seen before seized him and demanded to know where he had gotten the gold. Without warning, there were more Whites. They tied White Eagle to a table and began to beat him. 'Tell us where you got the gold or die,' they yelled as they punched him.

"Even through the blood covering his face, I could see White Eagle knew he had made a mistake in showing them the shiny rocks. I knew he would not tell them where they came from, even if it meant his life. 'Talk, tell us where it is,' one of the Whites said as he slashed him with his knife. White Eagle responded by spitting blood in his face. In anger, the White stabbed White Eagle in the stomach.

"In the confusion, I threw the White holding me to the ground and made my escape. Jumping on my pony and riding, I left all the pelts and horses and fled with only my life. It was as if they had caught the breathing sickness, but the Whites did not have to breathe or taste the golden rocks. All the Whites had to do is see the rocks and they went mad. Killing to take that which was worthless."

"Will you be able to resist the White man's disease? Or will you fall under the spell of the yellow rocks?" Pinchot asked Remone.

"I struggle with greed like every man does," Remone said. "Everyone wants more than they need."

As they rode up the trail, slowly ascending to the top, Pinchot explained to Remone why the Sioux believed their destiny was to become the greatest tribe of the plains. "Because of the Great Spirit's love for the Sioux, he has given us the buffalo, the Black Hills, and a path for us to follow. If we walk this path, if we make his will our own, we will not fail. He will provide for us, and we will grow both on the inside," said Pinchot as he touched his heart, "and as a nation." He waved his hand at the hills.

As they reached the crest of the mountain, Pinchot said, "Follow me into the heart of Mother Earth, but let us purify ourselves first."

They passed the trees where the bodies of many braves had been buried suspended in the air where marauding animals could not reach them. "The spirits of our ancestors rest here." Pinchot pointed to the skeletal remains. "We will hear what messages they might bring us this night." From the summit, they could see miles away into the valley where the smoke from the campfires in their village rose into the sky.

Pinchot had picked their campsite because the rock structures around it gave the campers a windbreak, and there was already a fire-pit. Pinchot built a fire and mixed an elixir he poured into a clay pot on the fire. Reaching into his pouch, he took the mushrooms he had brought and put them in the pot with the other herbs.

The flickering firelight danced on the massive boulders surrounding the campsite and, as the darkness grew, made them look as if they were coming to life.

"The spirits are among us," Pinchot said in a whisper as little beams of light flew around them.

"They look like fireflies to me," said Remone.

"Look closer and see if they speak to us."

Remone began to see things but thought it was just his imagination. But neither Pinchot nor Remone heard any voices from the spirit world.

"Sometimes they speak to us and sometimes not," said Pinchot.

"Maybe they don't have anything to say on this night," answered Remone.

The two looked at the stars, and Pinchot pointed out the constellations he knew and told Remone the stories he remembered about them. Their discussion grew deeper because Remone had many questions. For growing within Remone was the heart of a seeker with a desire for wisdom that could not easily be quenched.

Knowing that Pinchot was a brave of great faith in his beliefs, Remone asked him, "How do you know there is life after this one?"

"I believe the travail one endures in leaving this world is much like the travail we suffer being born into this world," said Pinchot. "A baby fights to stay in the warm, safe belly of his mother as long as possible, just as we fight to keep from dying, putting it off as long as we can. But there is something better on the other side for both the baby being born and for the one who dies. Just as the baby does not know what lies beyond the mother's womb, the old and sick ones do not know what lies beyond this life. Both changes are the result of growth. The baby grows too large to stay in the mother's belly, and the soul grows too large to stay in this world. It is like the brave who grows too large for the clothes he wore as a child. We outgrow our bodies. Then it is time to leave. Time to meet the Great Mystery."

They watched the shooting stars, leaving their traces across the horizon. On this still night with no wind, the whole universe seemed to be closer, pushing down on them, compressing them between the earth and the sky. They were aware of every sound. A whip-poor-will sang out its lonely soliloquy. The crunching sound of an animal stepping on a stick carried through the night air from a mile away. And then Remone strained his ears to hear a sound coming from the pine grove. *It sounds like running feet!* Pinchot spun into action, picking up a large limb from the firewood as four figures sprang into view in the firelight.

"What is white dog doing here in the most sacred of places?" Black Wolf screamed like a lunatic at Pinchot and Remone. He jumped forward and struck Remone in the face.

Pinchot used the limb to hit Black Wolf in the stomach, knocking the wind out of him.

The other Indians circled Pinchot and Remone, chanting, "Leave, betrayer of the earth." One leaped for Remone, but he, too, was felled by Pinchot.

The other two grabbed Remone and held him while Black Wolf spun and gave a flying kick to his chest, and with a sharp cracking sound, Remone collapsed face-first to the ground. Black Wolf laughed maniacally and yelled, "Eat dirt, white dog!"

Pinchot yelled, "Stop!" and charged the group of Black Wolf and his friends, but they had done the damage they had come to do. They ran laughing back into the night as Pinchot chased them. Their shadows disappeared into the darkness, their cowardly ambush accomplished.

Pinchot walked back toward Remone, who had gotten to his feet and wobbled toward the fire. "Are you hurt?" asked Pinchot.

"What the hell happened?" said Remone as he fell to his knees, holding a cracked rib.

Seeing this, Pinchot ran to help Remone to his feet.

"Owww, I think something is broken," moaned Remone.

"Let's get you over to the fire," Pinchot said, but this time, he reached for Remone's elbow and steadied him.

"How did they know we were here?"

"They must have followed our trail up the mountain. I think you have a broken rib. I am going to gather sticks and make a splint for you."

Pinchot wrapped Remone's ribs with wood and wove the sticks together, pulling them tight as Remone winced in pain.

"Yeah, maybe being here isn't the greatest idea for a White man," said Remone through his clenched teeth.

"It is Remone's right to be here. All may commune with Wakan Tanka, but maybe now is not the time."

All Remone wanted to do was get back to his teepee and away from this place.

12

Preserve your way of life,
the only life you know,
or strive for something better,
reaching up to the cosmos.

T HE WHITE MAN LOOKS AT time as something linear, always moving in a straight line, one event on top of another. Time moving from the past into the present. Progress is made as cities are built, wars are fought, and elections are won. Those seizing power are those whose names are destined to last as a dot on the timeline, their influence good or bad remembered.

The Indians see time as moving in cycles. This is shown in the use of the medicine wheel with the four-pointed cross in the middle symbolizing the four seasons and the direction of the four winds. The cosmos is represented in the sphere in which all events have been and will occur again. Everything is connected. All is in oneness in the Lakota Sioux's view of the universe.

"Dampen your senses so that your eyes might open wide," the shaman said, tapping the center of his forehead to emphasize where the third eye might open. "See beyond sight. Look deeper, deeper into your soul."

The young braves sat and listened to the shaman to learn the way of the enlightened one.

"Silence the noise of your own mind so that you might better hear the voice of the Great Spirit calling for you. Look at Canowicakte, the hunter of our people. Trained to see into the darkness and know where the herd lies, he covered his eyes in animal skins to increase the power of his inner vision. Canowicakte wanted to be a great hunter and lead the hunt. Closing one sense made his other senses stronger, but it was only during his vision quest on his sixteenth birthday that he was given what he sought. He gained the power of the great owl, Mas Mahapee."

"For many a night, he heard the hooting of the owl calling him to join him in his flight, 'Come, Canowicakte, and take this great leap of faith that we might be one. See through my old soul's eyes. Gain wisdom and inner sight to see through the darkness.' As a young brave, Canowicakte wanted what many young men desired in their vision quest, an animal of great valor able to tear the others apart and rule by might. The child in Canowicakte wanted a bear or a mountain lion to lead him and show him the path, not an owl who called for him. He wanted, as all braves do, a trial with which to brag to other braves of his passage. An owl calling him through the trees was not what he had envisioned. Still, the call was strong, and Mas Mahapee knew Canowicakte by name.

"Finally, after many nights of hearing the call at moonrise, Canowicakte answered in his heart, 'Yes, I accept your gift.' His soul and the owl's soul were as one as he flew with him to the top of the trees. They flew for many hours, which passed like minutes in Canowicakte's state of excitement. The light shone in the woods bathed in purple as the quarter moon waned in the sky.

"The owl needed to tell him nothing, as they were one. Canowicakte saw all the owl had ever seen through his eyes over many lives, as they were now part of his psyche. He felt the owl's need for sustenance to sustain his flight as if it were his own. Scouring the fields from on high, he spied a mouse and immediately descended through the dark as it scurried through the grass. He caught the mouse in his claws and carried it up into the trees. 'Thank you for nourishing me,' the owl prayed in thanks to the Great Spirit. 'To you I will give the gift of the hunt,' the wise old owl told Canowicakte. 'You will see beyond sight as long as you believe. If you lose faith, you lose all medicine. Remember, you must always give thanks for all living things that give their life to sustain you.'

"The young brave, eager to gain more knowledge and status in the tribe, agreed to the owl's terms. 'See, the sun is rising in the east. We must return.' They flew over the village where all were asleep in their teepees. A light snow covered the ground. Canowicakte looked down where he lay sleeping, lying on the stone bed where he had sweated himself to purification. He saw himself in his vision as he slept, entering back into his body, and he awoke the next day as if waking from a dream.

"The owl would lead Canowicakte into the hunt, always knowing where the bulls were. He quickly gained respect in the tribe. The others counted on him to find nourishment for the tribe even in the winter months. With his second sense, his visions would take him flying across the fields and streams, looking for venison or buffalo to feed his people. Then he grew pompous as Canowicakte saw himself as more than man but as god of the hunt. He gave no thanks to the Great Spirit or the animals whose lives were given to nourish the tribe. Nothing bent the knee of the prideful brave.

"As he grew further apart from the Great Spirit and his owl totem, he also began losing his second sight. His gift was in danger of going dark. He was tested the next winter when the tribe ran out of meat. With little grain or nuts left in the women's pots, the tribe grew thin. They called on Canowicakte to lead the hunt. Dread filled Canowicakte as he led the braves into the woods. They left many tracks in the snow, climbing the hills above the river and beyond. But he saw no place in the woods where deer wintered or sought food from eating tree bark.

"For seven days, he led the braves in the hunt, but each day they returned home with nothing. He fled the village, ashamed, for he knew it was his pride that had caused all to hunger. He took refuge in one of the caves where he had shelter from the wind and threw himself on the mercy of the Great Spirit. 'Please help me to humble myself to your will,' he prayed to Wakan Tanka.

"The next day, as he arose from his sleep, he saw a buck approaching the caves. Canowicakte slowly reached for his bow. The deer spoke, saying, 'The Great Mystery has sent me to help you feed the tribe. Only one arrow will you get to use.' With that, the deer turned to bound back into the trees, but Canowicakte's arrow found its mark midair while the deer sprang to clear a fallen tree.

"He put the deer on his back and headed back to the village. He was hailed as a hero as he carried the deer past the teepees. Still, he thought to himself, *Where is my inner sight? Why have the owl and the Great Spirit abandoned me?* At last, the owl, Mas Mahapee, spoke to Canowicakte again. 'You seek to gain that which you have lost. I warned you to give thanks and not presume your gift was something you would always have. You exalted yourself over the Great Spirit. I will show you the path, but you must strive to stay on it. You may walk in darkness because the trail is long and winding. Know that you do not have to stay in the dark but climb out to where the light of the Great Spirit can illuminate you instead. Your pride has blinded you. Humble yourself in the wilderness, where no man can see what you do. Fast and perform blood sacrifice before Wakan Tanka's eyes alone. Through abstinence, self-denial, and penance serving the tribe, you will regain favor,' the wise old owl counseled.

"'I will attempt to make myself worthy again,' said Canowicakte in a voice full of remorse as he nodded in agreement to the owl, the emissary of the Great Spirit. For weeks, no one in the village saw Canowicakte. He fasted and sustained himself only on berries and tree bark. He took a vow of silence to commune with the Great Spirit, piercing his flesh to do penance for losing his way. Then his loss of blood and lack of food caused him to lose consciousness, drifting into a dream state.

"In his vision, he flew with the owl high over the peaks of the Black Hills and down into the heart of the woodlands. There the owl took him to a gathering of animals. All the animals the Sioux hunted were gathered there and spoke to Canowicakte. The first was the Sacred Buffalo Cow. 'To you I give the sacred hunt. For all Sioux time, we have embraced you as lords of the plain. You have never wasted our flesh and we have bonded with you in the ritual of the hunt. But know that there is a sting in you not bending your knee in thanks to what we have given.'

"Next was the Great Matriarch Mother Doe of all Deer, who said, 'Many times I have seen you in the village of the Sioux, from the time you were a papoose suckling on your mother's breast to a young brave hunting in the woods. Now I have given you my children, perished to feed your tribe. All I would ask of you is your thanks for that which has sustained you in the circle of life.'

"All of the animals expressed themselves. The vision took the form of a trial, like a man might expect to experience in the afterlife when he answered for what he had done while alive. Canowicakte returned to the village a different man, forever changed, not superficially but deep into his being. In appearance, his fasting left him a thin ghostlike version of the man he had been, but from his eyes, a light shone that had not been there before. Now when he did speak, his voice and words resounded with authority. Now he gave thanks for the animal's lives that sustained his people. Before he had been something of a braggart, but now Canowicakte gave credit to the Great One."

"What lessons did Canowicakte learn in his journey?" the shaman asked the young braves.

"Dampening your senses makes the other senses stronger," said Chatan.

"Show you are thankful for all that you receive," said Chippewa. "For it is only through appreciation that one can fully enjoy what they have been given."

"Close all other paths except the one true path that has been chosen for you," said Tusca.

"Hear the true voice over all the noise of your mind," said Chenoa.

"Yes, very good," said the shaman. "And does the knife take credit for tearing the flesh or the one that holds the knife in his grasp? Even in this way, the Great Spirit who holds all of us within his grasp should be given honor for all that he does through us."

13

PINCHOT TOOK REMONE SEVERAL MILES downstream from where the village life bustled on the river. "Today, I will take you to where the big fish are. I had you bring your bow. We will see whether the hook or the arrow brings us the most fish."

The trail they followed meandered beside the river. Then a mountain stream added more water to the river, making it run faster. Pinchot motioned Remone to the left.

"Do you hear that?" said Pinchot, but his voice was nearly drowned out by the roar of water.

Pinchot and Remone ran down the sloping path to where the river increased its speed and dramatically dropped hundreds of feet. This was different from the nearly still river at the village. The mist that grew out of splashing water made it hard to see. Moss grew thick on the rocks and made them slippery to walk on.

They kept going until they came to a large pool of water. Pinchot jumped down to a large boulder where they could sit and see into the water. "We will see what we can do today," Pinchot said as he checked his pack.

Remone could see several large spotted trout resting where there was no current. Their golden hued scales sparkled in the sunlight as they bobbed gently up and down in the water.

"Here let us try with the line first," Pinchot said as he unwound the string.

"Here tie this on," Pinchot said as he handed Remone a sharpened quail bone to use as a hook.

Remone took the line and placed one end in his mouth to make it stiff with his saliva, making it easier to direct it into the hole that had been cut in the bone.

"That reminds me of my son," said Pinchot. "That is what he used to do when I would take him fishing."

"Oh," Remone looked up in surprise, "I didn't know you had a son."

"We used to hunt these woods every day."

"Where is he now?" Remone said without thinking.

With a sigh, Pinchot said, "He was taken from me in a hunting accident. Even now, it troubles me to talk about it." He turned away from Remone and stared into the sky, reliving a moment from his past.

"I am sorry, I did not know," Remone said and asked no more, but he could tell Pinchot carried a heavy weight from his loss. Silently he finished tying the string to his pole.

Pinchot turned back to face Remone and reached into his pouch, pulling out a variety of grubs, earthworms, and bugs. "Try this one," Pinchot said as he handed a large grub to Remone.

Remone hooked the grub and dropped it in the water as Pinchot watched. As Remone fished, Pinchot attached a thin line of buffalo sinew to his arrow. "I do not think they are hungry. We will see if this might work." He stood and gracefully hopped down, jumping from rock to rock until he was only a few feet above the water.

"The trick is to pull back hard on the bow so the line will not have any slack in it, or you will miss your shot," Pinchot said as he coached Remone and took aim. He checked the slack in his line before he inhaled and released his arrow. It sailed straight to its mark.

"Show me how to do that!" Remone said excitedly as he watched the fish wrestling with the line, rolling in the water, and trying to release himself. Remone hurriedly pulled his fishing line out of the water and wound it around his pole. He grabbed his bow and slid down to the rock where Pinchot was pulling his catch from the river.

"It is harder than it looks. Let me see your arrows," Pinchot said with a skeptical tone as he looked through Remone's quiver.

"This one looks good. See how it has a notch down at the bottom." Pinchot pointed to where there was a natural place to attach a string.

Remone nodded as Pinchot did all the work.

"Just add a little hole here," Pinchot said as he took his knife and, holding the arrow down on the rock, cut a hole just below the feathers.

"That should do it. Hand me some line from my pack."

Remone took out the dried buffalo line and pulled it straight, forcing the end through the hole in the arrow.

"That is good, now watch me tie the knot because you do not want it to be too loose. You do not want it to be wrong because it will affect the arrow's path," Pinchot said, using his years of experience as he pulled the line tight and tested it for Remone to see.

"Here let us see if you can feed the tribe tonight," Pinchot said as he handed the arrow back to Remone.

Remone stood up and imitated his mentor. He pulled back on the bow and shot into the pool, missing the fish. Time and again, he tried to shoot into the bed of trout, but all he did was scatter the school and cause them to look for safer water.

"It is not as easy as it looks. Is it?" Pinchot said to the disheartened Remone. "You have scattered these fish. We will have to move to another site."

"Let us go farther downstream," Remone said as shaded his eyes from the sun.

Jumping from rock to rock, the two fishermen looked for another still pool of water where fish might gather.

"Let us try here," Pinchot said, pointing to another deep pool of water.

Remone eagerly jumped on the rock and took aim.

"Go farther down so you can get closer to the water," Pinchot called to Remone.

Remone looked down at the rocks. They looked to be a good seven feet below him, so he tried sliding down on his butt, but before he could catch himself, Remone flew into the air and landed face-down in the pool of water.

As he came back up to the surface, Remone heard his teacher laughing. Always one who amused himself at Remone's expense, Pinchot's patience may have been tested if his student were not so entertaining.

"Get your bow. Do not let it get away!" Pinchot yelled to Remone.

"Wait, I'll have to dive for it now!" Remone said as he plunged in over and over again, looking in the depths for his bow.

Finally, Remone appeared back on the surface, bow in hand. He swam to the side of the river where he scaled the rocks back up to Pinchot. "That water is really cold even at this time of the year," Remone said as he shivered.

"Yes, your skin looks like it is turning blue," Pinchot said, teasing Remone. "I am the only fisherman here. Let us take our catch home and cook lunch."

14

"THE WHITES SPOIL THEIR CHILDREN because they want them to desire nothing," said the shaman, "but this does them no favor. In their bestowing of material things on their seed, they do not impart to them the lessons of life, leaving them to learn these lessons on their own. This understanding is much harder to learn as they turn into adults, their expectations and spirit often crushed in the process."

"Much better to learn these things as a child or young brave," Pinchot said. "When the sapling is green and will bend."

"The student often does not understand the purpose of the teacher's lesson," the shaman continued. "But the Great Mystery knows his plan for each of us. Consider the story of Yahato. Born blind, he was given up by his parents for others to raise, since his parents did not think they could care for him. Some in the tribe thought he should be left alone in the woods and let the wild animals have their way with him. But the old couple Mika and Tashima felt compassion when they saw the child. They knew they could raise him as their own. Being childless, they had yearned for a papoose of their own, but the years had advanced on them, leaving Tashima barren.

"As an elder in the tribe, Mika wanted to raise Yahato as a seer, a wise man to teach others the Sioux way. Raising him in this way often meant isolation for Yahato as a child as he spent his days listening to the elders. His isolation was more extreme because of his blindness. But he did not suffer the temptations or distractions the other braves faced. His mind, power, and soul grew unabated. In his solitude, he communed with the Great Spirit and called out his name. Because he did not have the noise of a hundred voices in his head, he was able to listen to the voice of the Great Mystery and heed his directions.

"When he reached puberty, it was discovered that Yahato had the gift of an inner eye. As he had developed no outer sight, his inner sight became more powerfully refined. His gift was discovered when Canow, the hunter, did not return to the village after going hunting. All asked what had happened to Canow.

"As Yahato slept, in his dreams, he saw Canow as he stalked a deer. It was as if Yahato was inside Canow's body and saw through Canow's eyes. He saw Canow as he crept through the woods down by the creek where the cottonwood trees grew. The deer loved to eat the bark from the trees. Careful not to step on any sticks, he silently moved in for the kill. Taking an arrow out of his quiver, Canow placed it on the bowstring and pulled it back.

"Suddenly, he heard something crashing through the brush behind him. He turned to see Mato, the brown grizzly bear, standing on his hind legs, roaring. The hunter had become the hunted! Mato swung his huge right arm catching Canow full force on his neck. Canow's head sailed through the air, a stream of blood spewing from his neck as his lifeless body collapsed to the ground.

"Yahato screamed out, 'Canow!' in his dream. He awoke to a teepee filling with villagers asking questions. 'We heard your cry. What has happened?' 'I have seen Canow. He is dead!' Skeptical faces looked at each other in the firelight of the teepee with one question on their lips, 'How are you, who is blind, able to see Canow?' 'In my dream, I have seen him fall,' answered Yahato. 'By the cottonwood trees on the creek bed, you will find his body. The great brown grizzly bear has taken his head from him. We must bury Canow with his head so he will have peace and not have to search for his head for all of eternity.'

"The next morning, the braves went to the creek only to find a half-eaten, badly decomposed body with no head. The bear had torn and eaten his body, but his quiver of arrows and the markings on his belt were unmistakably that of Canow.

"Soon Yahato's reputation spread over the Great Plains so that many Indians outside the village sought his counsel. Yahato had many visions and helped many of his people. Highly respected and sought out, Yahato had found his place in the tribe. Born without sight, he found that having less in the end gave him more," the shaman explained to Remone.

Later that same night, Remone lay in his teepee thinking about the shaman's words. Had he been raised as a spoiled White child? His thoughts returned to some of the stories he read when he was young. King Arthur with the royal Pendragon blood coursing through his veins was taken by Merlin to a poor farm family to raise him. The wizard was trying to bring up young Arthur in a setting where he would be given chores to do, learning the value of work and not treated as a prince who would grow up to be a monarch. His lessons in life would be harder, but he would learn to appreciate the lives of the common people in his kingdom. His humble upbringing would help him to become a great and just ruler.

Remone was beginning to think his time with the Sioux served the same purpose. The more he lived the tribal life—hunting, fishing, and doing the chores they required—the more he felt his old life fading away. The new Remone was becoming a more humble, introspective person. Because he had no choice, he did not have to rely on his own discipline to further his growth. He had the paths of his distractions closed, so only one path remained.

As he drifted to sleep, he began to dream. His animal sign, the turtle, came to him bearing a message. "Remone, you are still too selfish. Raised as a White child, you seek material things and want them immediately. Learn the patience of the turtle."

"But how can I depart from the ways in which I was raised? My thoughts are tied to my habits deep inside me."

"Slowly, through time, the Great Spirit has watched the journey of his people, often angered at the slow progress that has been made and the lack of patience that his children have had in learning their lessons," the turtle explained. "For man does not learn by words alone but also by the hand of nature coming upon him, like the waves of the ocean crashing on the mountains, tearing them down slowly blow by blow until they are turned to sand. Like water in the stream running over a stone, the water runs over it, wearing it down until it is smooth, honed into something worthy for the Great Spirit to use. Who are you to question the ways of the Great Mystery? Know the meaning of obedience from example of the great tortoise, Awana Ta, my great-great-great-grandfather."

The turtle exhaled a mist, filling the teepee so Remone could see his vision projected on the leather walls. Remone saw the story as if he were watching a movie. It was the story of the ancient turtles from the beginning of time slowly moving out of the safe shelter of their caves looking for a new home as ordained by the Great Mystery. The turtles struggled forward as the drying heat of the southern sun shriveled their shells. Then they took shelter in the mud during the day and waited until sunset before moving on in the cool night air to their destiny, slowly but deliberately. Many died as they moved forward until only one was left, the Great Awana Ta.

He advanced all the way to the Great Plains to what would someday be known as the Great Spirit's greatest creation of all, the Black Hills.

"I have brought you here to fulfill your destiny," the Great Spirit said. "Yours will be a great role to play in the universe."

"Here I am to serve my creator. What is it you would ask of your servant Awana Ta?"

"You must hold the weight of the heavens on your back, but you may choose the place. I will make the place you choose to labor from the most beautiful in the world, a paradise on earth."

"If I must remain unmoving under the weight of the sky, then I must choose a site on earth from which I can see. From the height of these hills, I can see all."

So the turtle's shell formed an island in the middle of the Great Plains from which the Black Hills grew. Between the earth and the sky, the turtle would hold the clouds in place and keep the world from being crushed.

Here Awana Ta formed the pillar of the universe. All turtles sprang forth as the children of Awana Ta. Wakan Tanka kept his promise to make the Black Hills the most beautiful site in the world.

The pine tree's roots encircled the turtle's shell and reached deep into the soil, helping Awana Ta to balance the heavy weight on his back. The shade of the trees invited all forms of animals and plants as streams formed, running down the mountains and joining the rivers flowing to sea.

The Lakota Sioux who called the Black Hills home grew into the greatest tribe of the plains. Their skill on horseback and with the arrow was without equal.

The Indians considered the hills magical. Through the centuries, the Sioux would talk of the strange rumblings coming from inside the Black Hills, but it was just Awana Ta shifting his shell to readjust his burden as he balanced the weight of the universe on his back.

15

REMONE AWOKE IN HIS TEEPEE in the morning, lying on the soft buffalo hide, thinking about his dream from the night before. His mind pondered many questions. He was starting to regret the life he had lived before he stumbled into the Sioux nation. Now he thought that previous life had been a waste of time and energy. He thought about the values the Sioux attached to all living things. All had a special place in the hearts of the Sioux.

Were the Sioux just superstitious, or could one look at the whole world in a way that all things were sacred? Was his falling into the river a sign from God that he should make changes in his life? What was the Great Mystery's plan for Remone?

Remone got up from his bed and escaped into the woods to contemplate these questions. He had never been a deep thinker. It hurt his head. He had never been thrust into a life-changing event like this. Before the pursuit of money was easier to understand. Now he saw that most White men straddled the fence between worshipping God and worshipping money. Money had been his god, even if he had been lazy and looked for shortcuts to obtain it.

The day passed as he wandered aimlessly in thought through the woods and up to the mountaintop where he sat and rested while he enjoyed the view. He could see the valley where braves on horseback were returning from the hunt. Smoke rose from the campfires where the evening meals were being prepared.

Returning to the village just before dusk, Remone looked for the shaman and found him talking to the young braves while he cooked his dinner by the fire. He had questions to ask him.

"I sense that you are looking for a sign from the Great Spirit to help you in finding your path," the shaman said to Remone without looking up from his cooking pot.

"It isn't that I am looking for a sign," said Remone. "It's that I don't know how to interpret the signs that I have been given."

"Some look for signs where there are none and read meaning into things where there is no meaning," said the shaman.

"What are you saying?" Remone asked with a puzzled look on his face.

"Look up into the sky," said the shaman.

Remone went to stand by the shaman as he used his staff to point. "What figure do you see in this cloud?" asked the shaman.

"Maybe a bear or a dog? Why? What do you see?"

"Only a cloud. I see only a cloud. I could use my imagination to see a shape, but it is man's mind that attaches meaning to shapes and looks for meaning where there is none. Men are constantly looking at everything as if it is a sign from the Great Mystery, but they are often in error."

"Like when my best friend got married and we all traveled to the wedding and the worst ice storm that ever occurred happened that night, right in the middle of spring. I considered this to be a bad omen. I looked for a sign within a natural event," Remone said. "But they are still happily married after many years."

"Some things are coincidence and that alone. Man reads miracles and meanings into these events, but in this, man is in error," said the shaman. "But to look at the cosmic order of the universe, the planets spinning through space, always in motion yet always in place, the earth and the way the moon stirs the tides, the changing of the seasons. For men who see all this and call it merely coincidence without recognizing the hand of the divine in it, *these* men are more in error."

16

THE YOUNG BRAVES BORROWED HORSES from their fathers to take camping. There were many skills to learn. Caring for the mares and their colts was among the chores all the boys performed. But the skills of shooting from a moving horse took training and practice. Pinchot assumed the role of teacher.

"Ride as fast as you can and release your arrow at this mark," said Pinchot as he planted his spear into the ground some sixty feet from the buffalo skin target. Tusca was the first of the young braves to take a shot. On his spotted Appaloosa, he charged up to the spear, but his hands were unsteady and unable to guide the horse and pull back on the bow at the same time. The galloping of the horse shook the arrow loose where it fell to the ground.

An embarrassed Tusca rode back to his laughing peers. But he had broken the ice for the rest of the braves. They knew that it was not as easy as it looked. They could do no worse than Tusca. The next up was Chippewa. Now Chippewa had more time on horseback than many of the other boys his age and had proven himself to be a good marksman. His arrow arched through the air and came down in the target. Although not a bull's-eye, the braves cheered for his effort.

"Practice will improve your aim," said Pinchot. "Chippewa has been upon a horse more than many of you. We will work until all of you will find this much easier to do."

Always one to teach by example, Pinchot leaped on Splitting Cloud and called out instructions as he rode. "Use your knees to guide the horse so that you can use both hands to pull back on the bowstring before you release the arrow. Then you will be ready to shoot!"

Straight and true, Pinchot's arrow found the bull's-eye, striking it with an impressive thud.

The young braves watched open-mouthed. They excitedly practiced until there was no daylight left.

"It is time for us to prepare dinner," said Pinchot as he turned his horse and led the braves back to the campsite.

The aroma of the deer Remone was cooking on the open fire welcomed the young braves back to their camp. After they had filled themselves with venison, the shaman asked them questions to make them think and grow as young men. "How do you see that your will and that of the Great Mystery are one and the same?"

"Keep a clear mind and an open ear to his voice," said Kiowa.

"Yes, good Kiowa. Focus on his voice through prayer," said the shaman.

"See that you grow as a warrior and in the skills of the hunt so that you will be ready," said Chippewa.

"Yes, for one must have the strength to answer the call of the Great Spirit and always be ready," said the shaman.

Hours later, the shaman shook the last ashes from his pipe and rolled out his bed to sleep. The boys took this as their cue that it was time to rest.

Remone and Pinchot stayed up and tended the fire.

"It is good that we are here. Are the braves learning new skills?" asked Remone.

"Yes, they are learning that it is much harder to shoot an arrow from a gallop." Pinchot laughed. "Today we drove the horses slowly. Tomorrow we will increase the speed of our attack. But it will not be as fast as when chasing the buffalo or in a fight with the Crow."

It was early morning when the young brave Tusca rode into camp, his horse panting, sweat dripping from his mane. "I have seen the Purple Buffalo!" Tusca shouted for all to hear. His excitement was visible as he abruptly turned his horse on its hind legs and charged back up the hill he had come down.

The other braves ran and mounted their horses. They followed Tusca galloping up the path to the mountain crest where they could see the buffalo on the plains below munching on the grass. Then down the hill, the braves charged, scattering the herd as they looked for one special bull.

Through the ravines and sagebrush they searched. The sun rose in the sky and the morning turned to afternoon, and still there was no sign of the Purple Buffalo. The buffalo were spent, as were the braves' horses. The herd stopped to eat grass again, as the braves talked amongst themselves and gave their horses time to rest.

"I have seen no Purple Buffalo," said Kiowa. "I think Tusca imagined it."

"Too much time filling his pipe," Chippewa said as he laughed and mimicked Tusca smoking his pipe.

"I have had enough, there is no Purple Buffalo here," said Chatan as he reached for his horse's reins.

"I am starving. It is time to see what is on the fire," said Chenoa as he leaped onto his horse. "Where is Tusca?"

But Tusca did not hear their talk. He was still mounted, combing the countryside, looking through the thickets and creek beds to flush out the Purple Buffalo. His fellow braves left him to hunt by himself. It was not until sunset and darkness began to fall that a weary Tusca slowly rode his horse back into the camp.

The other braves laughed at him. "Why do you still hunt for that which does not exist? You could be eating with us and warming yourself by the fire."

The shaman saw the tired brave riding into camp alone and heard the braves' taunts and shouted in an angry voice, "Tusca still hunts because he believes in the Purple Buffalo! He believes because he has seen him face-to-face! It is hard for those who have not seen to continue the chase."

17

THE SIOUX BELIEVED THAT ANIMALS were the harbingers of the Great Spirit. They brought them messages from the spirit world, and from those tidings, they learned what the Great Mystery wanted them to do. The Sioux like to don the animal's skin and believed by doing so they would truly become these animals, allowing them to take on the power of the animal.

Pinchot told the tale that once there was a marauding brown grizzly bear named Mato rampaging through the Sioux nation. "The bear had gone mad and grew to desire man's flesh," explained Pinchot. "No one dared to stop the bear, so knowing that I stood well with Wakan Tanka, I went into the woods to pray. After communing with him from morning to nightfall, the answer came from the Great Spirit, saying, 'Go, Pinchot, warrior that you are, and put on the skins of the black cougar for a disguise. Follow the bear back to his dwelling, and there you may lay your trap for him.'

"So I put on the cougar hide. The night was dark, but my animal totem, the cougar, gave me his eyes to see with. The trail of the brown grizzly Mato was easy to follow, his great frame left broken branches and mighty paw prints in the mud. But the bear was a trickster and spread the blood of a slain brave around a coyote den, leading me to think the coyotes had taken the brave's life.

"I followed Mato's trail into his lair deep in a forest cave. Checking my arrows to make sure the points were sharp, I slowly and quietly crawled on all fours, like a cougar, into the cavern. I was surprised to find a meeting of the woodland animals in the great chamber of the cave. Soon the animal voices let me know the brown grizzly Mato was the only one responsible for the deaths. Coyotes were there, asking, 'Why have you tried to make us the ones to be blamed for that which you do?'

"The grizzly bear laughed loudly and said, 'Have you not attacked men but always in packs? You are cowards to attack with many, while I do it alone.' 'Why have you been hunting man flesh?' the elk asked. 'Because there are too many of them,' said Mato, growling his answer. 'They take our food and wander onto our land. And because they taste good, I mean really, really good.'

"The great owl spoke, saying, 'Your heart is full of hate, and it is eating away at your soul.' 'You have no control over me. I am a bear and bigger than any of you and I will do as I choose!' the bear said in a voice that thundered. 'Look,' said a coyote, 'the cougar is here. What say you?'

"All of the animals looked at me in the shape of my animal totem. I leaped into action, jumping up with my bow, and shot an arrow straight into the bear's chest. The bear roared and charged across the cave, but with a second arrow, I stuck again at the bear's evil heart, but it took a third arrow to bring the bear down. The animals in the cave all cheered, and the owl cawed out, 'The great cougar has enacted a judgment on Mato whose path was wet with blood.'

"My animal sign, the cougar, had served me well once again," explained Pinchot. "The power I gained from being in the cougar's body helped me to restore justice and rid the woods of a violent threat. The cougar's eyesight that could see into the darkness was hard to give back. But I had to return to my people, knowing I would call on my ally again when I needed him."

18

THE SHAMAN OFTEN DEALT WITH the bereaved who were having problems accepting the loss of a loved one. One of these braves, Paytah, had recently lost his grandfather. They were very close, and the grandfather had given him a gift he had worked on for a long time. A beautiful talisman carved out of buffalo bone. The grandfather told Paytah, "With this talisman, you shall not want for food, for it will always point the way back to the buffalo from whence it came."

He showed Paytah how to suspend it in the air so it would point. "That is the way you would go, to the hunt!" his grandfather said excitedly.

The old man, not wanting to be a burden to his family, decided, it was time to go and meet the Great Mystery. He went to the medicine wheel high on the mountaintop above the village. There he asked the Great Spirit to take him away. Not wanting to soil the sacred place, he slipped down to the crest of the mountain where the view was a beautiful one—the last his eyes would see. Then as often happened, the animals of the woods helped speed up the meeting between man and deity. They devoured his body, leaving little to remain.

The shaman was talking to Remone when they overheard Paytah talking to the other braves. "It is not that my grandfather left us but how he left that hurts me! Taking his own life. How could he have gone and not told me goodbye? For that I cannot forgive him. How could he have gone in this way? He denied us a funeral in which we could honor him. I would have built his scaffolding high into the sky, in the tallest trees we could find, but his flesh is so torn now. There is no body left! How can his soul find its way to the spirit world? No,

I can never forgive him!" said Paytah. In anger, he took the talisman his grandfather had made and threw it deep into the woods.

"Paytah, we all experience loss," the shaman said. "It is how we learn to deal with it that takes us from child to man. It is up us to free our heart and grow, not take the wrong path down into darkness. We must all learn to forgive, though it is not easy. It cleans the slate of our heart so we can move on. Consider Pinchot, one we all respect. Pinchot rarely speaks of his wife, Chante, but did you know she died shortly after giving birth to their son, Tawachi? Pinchot raised Tawachi to be a great hunter like himself. The gift his wife left him of his son made Chante's death easier to bear and made Tawachi even more precious to him. Pinchot watched proudly as his son grew.

"Tawachi became a fine young brave," the shaman continued. "I remember when he returned from one of the raids on the Crows. Pinchot had led the raid, and they returned with many horses. Tawachi claimed a good-looking brown pony for his own. Learning to care for his horse, Tawachi matured and took great pride in his horsemanship. The annual spring races among the braves took place with four laps around the village. The whole tribe turned out to watch and cheer for the young braves.

"Many thought Ohanzee would win the race, as he was older and had been on a horse longer than Tawachi. During the first three laps, Ohanzee was in the lead with Tawachi close behind. The other braves fell behind until the race became a competition between just Ohanzee and Tawachi. In the fourth and final lap, Ohanzee's horse stumbled, and Tawachi cleared the finish line ahead of Ohanzee. I will never forget the look of pride on Pinchot's face as the tribe cheered for his son, Tawachi.

"I played a role in Tawachi's growth into an adult and taught all the boys my philosophy of life and the arts of healing. But Pinchot was the one who taught his son, along with the other young braves, the skills of the hunt. Skill with the bow and arrow was critical to providing food for the tribe. Pinchot taught the young braves how to pull back on the bowstring. 'Hold your breath as you take aim. Find your target and take your time. Do not breathe out until the arrow is released. This will make the arrow stable in its flight,' said Pinchot as he released his arrow straight into the target.

"All the braves progressed in their lessons but none so much as Ohanzee, who was Tawachi's best friend. Always practicing, he became very accurate with the bow, and his stealth in pursuing his quarry made him admired by the other braves. He excelled in providing food for the tribe. Together Tawachi and Ohanzee roamed the woods and hillsides, hunting and perfecting their aim with the arrow. One morning, while out tracking, Ohanzee knelt and pointed out, 'Deer tracks. Go around the hill and see if you can flush them out.' Ohanzee motioned to the left side of the hill. Tawachi nodded and silently started out.

"Tawachi worked his way around the hill and came up on a family of deer, a big buck, a doe, and two little fawns, all nibbling on the spring grass that was coming to life. He crept closer with his eye on the big buck. Slowly he pulled an arrow from his quiver and placed it on the bowstring. But the buck heard or smelt something and raised his head and stood at attention. Tawachi stopped moving and watched until the buck went back to eating. Tawachi started forward, eyes on the deer. His next step was onto a twig, which snapped loudly. The buck nosed the fawns, and the deer ran away with Tawachi chasing them.

"The deer ran out into the clearing, but Ohanzee was not ready, and the deer ran past. Then he saw a rustling in the thicket and was sure it was a fifth deer. He let an arrow fly, hitting Tawachi in the neck. Tawachi rose from the brush with the arrow sticking in his throat and, in his last breath, cried out, 'Ohanzee, what have you done?'

"I had the sad task of telling Pinchot," the shaman continued. "Pinchot dropped his head in his hands and sat sobbing. Then he disappeared. For many days, Pinchot was not seen in the village. He had gone to be alone, to ask the Great Spirit for the strength to sustain him through his great loss.

"After losing weight on a diet of berries and water alone, a weaker, frail Pinchot felt the Great Spirit wanted him to return to the village. As he walked past the teepees, he saw women out doing their chores but no men. He asked Amber Moon when he saw her,

'Where are all the braves?' She pointed to the council hall and said, 'A big meeting of the tribal council.' Pinchot knew why the tribal council was meeting. His calling by the Great Spirit to return to the village could not have been more well timed.

"'Ohanzee must pay for his crime,' said the men of the village. He stood before Chief Slow Bull and the whole tribe as they decided what his punishment should be. When Pinchot walked into the council hall, a collective gasp from the braves showed their surprise at Pinchot's return. Pinchot's emaciated condition and the look on his face told the council how he had suffered. Ohanzee shook with fear, afraid to face Pinchot.

"Pinchot walked to the front of the council and addressed Chief Slow Bull, 'May I speak to the council?' A stunned chief, rarely speechless, looked at Pinchot with pity and motioned for him to speak. 'For many days, I have struggled within my spirit between anger and sorrow,' said Pinchot. 'At first, I wanted Ohanzee's blood to be spilt, just as my son's blood had flowed. I imagined my hands snapping Ohanzee's neck like an oak sapling, twisting it until it would grow no more.' Pinchot did a twisting motion with his hands as anger distorted his face.

"The council could see the conflict going on inside Pinchot as his face grew calm again. 'Then the Great Spirit came to me and soothed my tortured soul. For many nights, I communed, seeking the answer, until I knew the path the Great Spirit wanted me to choose. Now I know that what Ohanzee did was an accident. Please do not take his life.'

"Pinchot turned to face Ohanzee and reached into his pouch. The young brave recoiled in fear as Pinchot pulled out a knife skillfully carved from bone. 'Here, Tawachi would want you to have this. It was one of the last things he made. Let this gift be a bond between you and me so that you will know I bear you no ill.'

"A sobbing Ohanzee fell to his knees and hugged Pinchot's feet. 'I am sorry. I have lost my best friend, Tawachi. And it has been at my own hands a weight I will carry for all time.' 'I know and that should be punishment enough to satisfy this council,' Pinchot said as he gazed around the council chamber and looked each brave in the eye. Chief Slow Bull rose and spoke. 'If Pinchot can forgive, can this council do less? I say we give Ohanzee his freedom.'

"The tribe nodded their approval. By forgiving Ohanzee, Pinchot had freed himself from some of the pain he carried from his son's death," the shaman explained.

Later, outside the council walls, the shaman explained Pinchot's action to the young braves. "Forgiveness frees one's heart from being roped to the wrong you were done." The young braves looked on in disbelief as they listened. "Forgiveness allows your healing to begin."

Hearing Pinchot's story made Remone think about his family back home, back to that fateful day when an intruder had broken into his farmhouse and stole his guns. Uncle Ed returned home without knowing his house had been violated and was an easy victim for the thief, who ambushed Ed with a fireplace poker and took his life.

The murderer fled, but the authorities caught him at a roadside bar across the state line. He was drunk and bragging about the money he was going to make selling the guns and how stupid the homeowner was to come in and surprise him. One of the people in the bar took him seriously enough to call the police. The police found he had left Uncle Ed's station wagon with the windows open. In the passenger seat was Ed's wallet. The guns that had been stolen were covered with a tarp in the back.

The evidence was incriminating. Remone remembered a feeling of satisfaction when the felon had been caught. *I may have lost my uncle, but at least they got the bastard. I hope they fry his ass!*

But Remone's feelings turned to shock when he learned his cousins had met with the murderer in prison. They met with him and prayed, forgiving him for his crime. Remone's cousin Kathryn told him, "I want to see you walking the streets of paradise with me when you come to know Jesus."

Remone thought they were crazy. But theirs was not fake religion. To be able to forgive someone who murdered your father was not something he could do. He wished he had a god like theirs in his life.

It took many days of searching through the woods for something someone had lost. But when Remone finally found it. He looked for Paytah; he had something to return to him.

"Paytah, I found something of yours," said Remone as he placed the talisman around his neck.

Paytah embraced Remone. "Thank you so much, I threw this away in anger. It has troubled me. This was the last gift my grandfather gave me."

"I knew you threw it away in anger. I know what it is to make a mistake because of one's anger," answered Remone. "But to deal with grief, one must forgive and hold onto those things that remind you of the person lost. I knew that you would want the talisman to help you remember your grandfather."

19

REMONE WAS HAVING A BAD dream. He was back at the real estate office on a Monday morning, stuck in front of a computer screen. His back was stiff from sitting in his uncomfortable office chair. The fluorescent light flickered and buzzed overhead. He knew it was a beautiful spring day outside, but there was no window in Remone's office, just the horrible smell of mold growing in the walls from a leak in the ceiling that Gant had let go unrepaired.

He felt like a fly on a sheet of fly paper—small and insignificant. Sacrificed to build the real estate empire that Gant dreamed about.

Mr. Gant called over the intercom, "Remone, have you forgotten about our meeting? It's time for your six-month review. Bring your sales report with all the prospects you have been talking to. My office. Now!"

It was all coming back to him as he walked down the hall to Mr. Gant's office. Remone hated his job. He knocked on Gant's door and felt a tightening in his gut that he hadn't felt in a long time. The anxiety set in as Mr. Gant barked, "Come in, Remone."

Gant sat without looking up from his desk as he shuffled papers. "Have a seat, Remone. Do you know why you're here?"

"Well, I guess it's time for my six-month review."

Mr. Gant leaned forward in his chair, putting his face less than a foot from Remone's. "You haven't had a sale or set up a listing in over two months."

"Has it been that long?" Remone said, rubbing his chin while he played dumb.

Gant's face took on a red hue as he brought his fist down on the desk. "Hell yeah, it's been that long. That's why I am going to write you up and put you on probation, Remone," Mr. Gant said with a growl. "You're just not getting the job done, Remone."

"Wait a minute, Mr. Gant! I think you're overreacting," said Remone as he struggled for words.

This only made Gant angrier as the veins on his head bulged. "Overreacting?"

Gant's face tightened so much around his mouth Remone thought he might swallow his tongue.

"I'll show you overreacting. Here's what I want you to do. I want you to come up with an action plan on how you're going to pull your business out of the toilet. You're going to make at least fifteen calls a week to get listings. I don't care if you do it at night when the owners get home or if you do them all on the weekends. I will follow up with you every Monday morning and every afternoon before you leave."

"But don't we already have a Monday morning sales meeting?"

"We'll meet just before the staff meeting, Remone. Just you and me. I want you to come in before everybody else. And use this lead tracking report. Any questions?"

For a split second, Remone wished Mr. Gant's heart, if he had one, would explode right there in front of him. Gant's face would tell it all—a look of surprise mixed with horrific pain. His last words, "Oh shit," would summarize a life spent in the pursuit of greed. He would know it was the end, grabbing his heaving chest and taking his last breath as the paramedics stumbled through the door, too late to help.

But Remone snapped out of his fantasy. "No, I guess that's all pretty clear, Mr. Gant," he said through clenched teeth.

Damn, thought Remone. *Now I am really screwed. I get to spend all my time filling out paperwork and in meetings instead of selling.* He slammed his office door shut and slid back into his chair.

Violent thoughts flashed through Remone's mind. Things he could do with his hunting rifle other than killing deer. How long would Mr. Gant survive if he was naked and afraid in the wilderness with Remone stalking him. Remone might fire a few shots close enough to scare him and make him run faster through the woods. Remone might yell out, "Hey, Gant, who's in charge now?"

Remone smiled to himself. He pictured Gant's white butt cheeks moving together as he cowered behind a tree for cover from Remone's hail of bullets. He would try to distance himself from Remone, but Remone would pursue him, and he knew how the hunt would end—with Gant's lifeless body draped over the truck. Remone and his hunting buddies would pose for pictures, rifles in hand, smiling with pride at their trophy from the hunt. And Remone would have a new picture to show off on his office wall.

Remone smiled in satisfaction at his daydream, but there were the authorities and jail time for his indiscretions. He pictured in his mind the staff at the real estate office being interviewed on the local news.

"He was such a nice guy. I could never have pictured him doing this. I had no idea he was so disturbed," Sarah would say, tossing her red hair for the television cameras.

"I always knew Remone was a bad seed. He wasn't much of a realtor either, too lazy. It's a shame about Mr. Gant, such a great man," Stella would say in her dry personality.

And there would be a trial. Remone pictured a trial by jury, with the prosecution calling out for the death penalty. Remone's attorney would argue for life in prison and say it was a crime of passion.

Remone alone would know the truth, that he really enjoyed killing Mr. Gant and would enjoy doing it again and again. But Remone's attorney would win.

Remone would be led out of the courtroom and taken to the West Des Moines ERA Real Estate office. He would be led to a little office in the back with no window and a noisy flickering fluorescent light in the ceiling. The officers would chain him to his desk for the rest of his life. Forever!

Remone squirmed on his buffalo hide bed as the nightmare continued until he heard Pinchot at the teepee door. "Is the great hunter Remone awake?"

A feeling of relief shot through Remone's body. *It was only a dream!* And he realized he was still in the Sioux nation and not back in the realtor's hell.

"You do remember that we were going hunting today?" asked Pinchot.

Remone jumped to his feet. "Yes, I am ready." He grabbed his bow and quiver of arrows and came out of the teepee, eagerly greeting the day.

Today Pinchot took Remone out to shoot quail. The wind blew gently through the tallgrass like waves across the ocean.

"It is a most beautiful day, the sun gently kisses Mother Earth in celebration of spring," Pinchot said as they searched a creek bed for pheasant.

"I am glad it is warmer," said Remone as he plucked his bowstring.

"The maids are starting to bathe in the river," Pinchot said with a laugh.

"Now, Pinchot, you haven't been sneaking a peek at those girls, have you?"

"Every now and then, I have stumbled upon them."

"But you didn't stumble back out until you had gotten a good look?" Remone teased.

"I have seen Amber Moon's eyes on you."

"But have you seen her bathing..."

Suddenly, Pinchot held out his hand. "Shhhh." He pointed over to a fat quail waddling through the tallgrass, pecking at the ground for something to eat. To bring down a deer was enough of a challenge and could be done at some distance, but with a prey as small as a quail, one needed to move in closer for the shot to be accurate. They crouched on the ground as they slowly closed the distance on their quarry.

Remone and Pinchot both drew back on their bows, taking careful aim and letting their arrows fly at the same time.

Remone couldn't contain himself and let go a wild shout, "Bingo!" as he leaped into the air and ran over to the dead bird, picking up the trophy and dancing in a circle.

Pinchot silently pointed to Remone's arrow stuck in the sand some distance in front where the bird had fallen. They began laughing as Pinchot slapped Remone on the back. "You should have seen your face," Pinchot said as he imitated Remone's wild dance.

20

The auras are as a weathervane
of the soul,
from which one can tell
which way the winds of destiny blow.

T HE SIOUX PRACTICED MANY RITUALS that were designed to change their state of cognizance—from holy men putting themselves into trances to visit the spirit world to taking different plants and herbs to achieve a heightened sense of consciousness. This was a serious pursuit for the braves passing into manhood.

From his first meeting with the Shaman, Returns Again, Remone had heard of the auras. He had asked Pinchot, "What is the shaman seeing when he talks of the auras?"

"I have seen the colors, but you must ask the shaman yourself," answered Pinchot.

Crossing the village, Remone found the shaman helping one of the families of the village. Here he was helping a young maid who was having cramps associated with her maturing into a woman.

"Take the mugwort plant with some sage and mash it until it is soft," the shaman said as he demonstrated using his stone knife. "Then boil it and let it steep so that you can drink it like a tea. Do this twice a day, and she will feel better."

After waiting for his turn to approach the shaman, Remone asked, "Tell me about the auras that you see."

"What would you like to know?"

"What are you seeing when you talk of seeing the auras?"

"The colors that all things have within them. You as a White would have a hard time slowing your mind enough to see them."

"Then how can I see them?" Remone persisted.

"I can show you, but we must make ready. On the next crescent moon, we will gather and Remone will see the colors."

Remone doubted if most people believed in auras, but he knew the people he worked with at the real estate office wouldn't spend the time to look for them. He had heard people talk about meeting someone who had a strong or attractive aura. He thought they meant that the individual just smiled brightly and had a good attitude that came shining through. But they weren't saying they had seen colors coming out of the top of their heads.

Remone had vacationed abroad and had been to the great cathedrals and art museums of Europe. He had seen many of the great paintings by Donatello, Michelangelo, and Raphael. The painters depicted Christ, the Madonna, and other saintly figures with halos firmly planted on their heads. *Maybe these were the auras as they had been seen in olden days?*

The days passed, and the night of the crescent moon was to come. He was more than curious. Remone had a growing thirst for knowledge. Remone eagerly went about his chores and ate his dinner quickly so he could gather with his Indian brothers in the ceremonial tent. The shaman and several others were already there when Remone entered and found a place to sit across from Pinchot.

"All things alive and dead have a vibration reflected in colors," the shaman began. "Whether it is animal or plant. It can be a stone that once was alive. All have a vibration and a color to go with the note it plays. Don't look for the auras under the bright light of the noonday sun, but rather you will see the soul's inner light when you are least expecting it. There is no need to strain your eyes," the shaman said as he pushed the cacti into the ceremonial pipe.

"Remone will see things more clearly after this night," Pinchot said as he lit the pipe and inhaled deeply.

The tent walls danced in the flickering firelight as Remone drew a breath of the mescal cactus deep into his lungs. Some of the other participants started beating out a slow rhythm on their drums. One could hear the beat of Mother Earth's heart in the Sioux drums. The shaman pushed at the hot coals with a stick, which he used to relight the pipe, and then passed it on.

"Tonight, we will look on the colors that are all around us and the signs these colors can tell us about ourselves, both skills and weaknesses," said the shaman.

Pinchot pointed at Remone and said, "I see the sign of the turtle."

"Yes," said the shaman. "Remone will draw his strength and insight from the turtle, for he shall move slowly but very deliberately, never rash or impetuous in his decisions as he carries the weight of the world upon his back. He must learn to be steady."

"I just feel like I am moving at the speed of a turtle after smoking this stuff," Remone said as he steadied himself.

"Remone's aura has changed as he lives with us in the Sioux nation," said the shaman. Now I see in Remone the colors of the seeker, violet and indigo, as he continues his journey of discovery. Remone's soul has grown. I see his destiny is to become a real human being."

"I often see Pinchot's red aura when he is preparing for the hunt. His sign is the cougar. He gains his strength from him and helps to feed the village, but tonight Pinchot's aura is purple as he seeks oneness with the Great Spirit," said the shaman.

Pinchot just smiled and rocked back and forth, sitting cross-legged before the fire.

"Look into the fire more deeply, look more deeply into your soul," chanted the shaman in his ancient voice.

Remone's head grew dizzy. His heart jumped in his chest as he looked across the fire and saw the Great Black Bear roaring! His friend, Heart of a Bear, was standing on two legs, wobbling as he swung with his two great claws. As he looked, the animal vision passed away, revealing only Remone's friend with luminous colors in a deep blue hue coming out of his abdomen. The mood in the tent started to change as the braves sat and listened. Remone blinked and wiped the sweat from his forehead as the hallucinations came and went.

"Through my visions, I have seen Remone as he lived in the White man's world," the shaman muttered. "You were tangled in the White man's web, sitting and working in his house of stone day after day. The only time you went outside was going to meet other Whites, riding in the carriage without horses. You sold bits of Mother Earth like it was something you could own."

"How can one sell that which is sacred?" Pinchot said, questioning what he heard.

"You lived in a smelly, noisy world," the shaman continued. "The sound from all the White's voices was enough to drown out the true voice of Wakan Tanka. How could you live in such a place?"

The tent swirled as Remone slipped into unconsciousness. Falling into a deep dream state, he felt himself descend into darkness. Remone dreamed as he fell deeper and deeper. He felt like he had fallen into a tar pit as he wrestled to free himself. Dark shadows reached out to pull him deeper into the mire. He couldn't move his legs, and there was a ringing in his head and nausea in his gut. Struggling to breathe, he looked up from his abyss and gasped.

The shaman sat cross-legged on a cloud. His lips moved, but Remone could not hear what he was saying. His eyes were closed, and he appeared to be praying. Then suddenly, a third eye opened on his forehead, and a purple violet beam of light shot down into Remone's face.

"You look for more powers and search to discover the mysteries of the mind," the shaman called out to Remone. "But think of the wonders that already exist. They are at your arm's reach. Through your sight, you see the beauty of this world. With your tongue, you can tell others your thoughts. Through your love, you can produce another human being. These are the amazing gifts we have been given. The miracle of life is more magical than any magic the shaman can conjure. Yet we search and lust for more power. Use what you have to receive more."

Then with his third eye, the shaman drew Remone from the chasm and slowly raised him up into the sky just beneath the cloud he floated on. A shooting star crossed the horizon overhead as the shaman said, "Look at the stars, Remone. We take them for granted because they come out every night to reveal their beauty to us. If they only lit the sky once every hundred years, we would all stare in astonishment. But their beauty is there for *all* to see on any clear night. To never stop and look on them with amazement is true blindness."

Remone felt a true sense of awe as he absorbed the lesson of his teacher. A fullness filled his soul that he had never felt before.

"Remone, open your inner eye and see the skills and powers that you already possess."

As the shaman spoke, Remone's third eye opened. He could not just see with the sight he had gained. Remone found he could feel with it. Remone felt a sense of gratitude for his life, and he knew he had to use it because it was only a loan from the Great Mystery. It was a gift that he could choose how to use while he was still alive.

Awaking from his vision, Remone took the lesson with him and found a new respect for the shaman's powers, knowing that he could not only interpret but also enter his dreams.

21

A COOL SPRING BREEZE RUSTLED the limbs of the trees where the birds sat and added their song to the lessons the shaman taught the young braves. "Where is the worth of a man found?" asked the shaman. "Is it in battle? Or is it in the hunt and bringing back food to feed our people?"

"The value of a man lies in his honor, in his words ringing true because his actions support his words," said Pinchot.

"Well said for the one who leads the hunt," the shaman said, smiling at Pinchot as he continued. "Many men mean to speak the truth but because of their lack of action are found to have a crooked tongue. What else gives a man value?"

"My boss used to say, money is the only measuring stick," said Remone.

The shaman sighed and replied, "Once a great snake came into the Sioux village eating all the mice in the field where corn had been planted. Then he began eating all the birds as he slithered through the trees, becoming fat, and *still* he kept eating! 'I am not really hungry, but I do not want anyone else to eat my share,' the large snake was heard to say.

"As fat as he had gotten, he tired and stopped by a brook to sun on a big rock. Without warning, the shadow of an eagle covered the ground. But because of his extra size and weight, the snake could not slither to the reeds before he was caught in her talons. The eagle called out a message to the animals of the forest. 'Stay hungry,' she cawed out as she carried off the snake to feed her young nursing in her nest."

"But what does this mean other than saying greed weighs all of us down, making us fat?" Remone said. "The more things you own, the more work you have to do to keep them."

"You know nothing of the shaman's words!" said Pinchot, admonishing Remone. "The snake is the White man. His hunger is ever gnawing at his stomach. He devours all he sees with an unquenchable appetite, consuming everything and leaving nothing. You cannot escape from his great greed!"

Hours later, Remone lay in his teepee, thinking about what the shaman had said. His thoughts drifted back to when he was a teenager. His friends talked about philosophy, art, and dreams of the future. They lived in their parents' homes and had not yet joined the White man's race to obtain. They were not weighed down with years of chasing money. Greed had not yet consumed their souls and all their time and energy.

As he drifted to sleep, he dreamed of his old life in the real estate office, scrambling every day to keep his deals sown together, with him drinking every night to help him cope with the stress. If he could just get his deals closed faster, he would have more—more status, bigger cars, more expensive suits, and more toys. More. He just wanted more.

"Remone, there is *more* to life than simply increasing its speed," said his animal guide, the turtle. His animal totem, the turtle, had returned to speak to Remone through his dreams.

"Moving slower allows you to see more, take in more, enjoy more, and be more. Slow your life down to a *crawl*. Try to approach cosmic time where life becomes so magical that time itself seems to stand still.

"The White man is obsessed with owning. He has to own everything. It is a concept the White man has created, which the Red man will never understand. Does the eagle flying high in the sky seek to own all he surveys, or is it enough to experience being a part of all creation? Taking back time is the greatest gift anyone can give themselves, but it is up to you to do this. No one can do it for you. See that you do not waste your time. The Great Spirit arranged the universe to remind you of the passing time. The seasons, the four winds, and clouds floating across the sky. The setting of the sun and moonrise all mark the days as they vanish from sight."

Remone awoke in a sweat. He felt a sense of relief seeing the familiar teepee walls. A restlessness in his spirit pushed him to get outside to walk and think. The fire smoldered, and he took a seat on the large fallen tree and looked up at the stars.

I am so glad to be here and not in my old life stuck in the office under the pressures of that world. As he sat by the fire, smoking his pipe, Remone thought he saw someone approaching him. *I thought the whole village was asleep.*

"I brought you hot tea," Amber Moon said as she bent over to hand it to Remone and turned away.

"Stay with me and talk," said Remone as he moved so she had room to sit. It was so different from talking to the shaman and Pinchot with their constant challenging. Amber Moon's presence alone gave a solemn quietness to the night. They had always been able to communicate without words. Remone thought they had a gift. The warm air blew through the village as the coals in the fire flickered, begging to burn again before dawn.

22

WALKING UP THE TRAIL, REMONE heard the crows cawing loudly from the woods but thought nothing of it.

The shaman heard something more. "There is a bear hunting in the woods, be careful."

As they continued walking, Remone saw a dark shape moving on all fours, stalking the grove of trees next to their trail.

"This way," said Pinchot, pointing up the trail. "Do not let him pick up our scent."

The three hurried up the hill far enough away to rest for a moment. "How did you know about the bear?" Remone asked the shaman.

"The birds told me. They called out a warning."

Remone remembered hearing the crows cawing but had thought nothing of it. The three men sat and unpacked their lunch.

"How does the White man hear messages from his god?" the shaman asked Remone.

"We go to church and the priest tells us what God's message is for us," Remone answered.

"You mean you do not talk to your god yourself?"

"No, I have not heard his voice myself," said Remone. "But we can read his messages from the great book, our Bible."

"And who has written this book?" asked the shaman.

"Well, men wrote this book, but it is God's words."

"How do you know these things?"

"It is what I was taught," answered Remone.

"Did the men that wrote the book see the things they tell about in the book?" asked the shaman.

"Some of the things that are told, they witnessed. But other stories and truths were told to them."

"How do you know these tales to be true?"

"They are like the Sioux legends," said Remone, who was losing patience. "Whether the stories are true or not, one can still learn from these lessons."

"Very good. Well answered, White man," the shaman said, smiling at Remone. "We are not taught to question the way we think. But it is something we should all do. It might change the conclusions we come to."

"Well, how do you think God speaks to you?" asked Remone.

"The animals tell me much. They are the emissaries of the Great Spirit, but I have trained myself to listen. I think the Whites spend no time to listen. They are so busy searching for money they have no time to discover the riches of their own hearts."

"I know what it is to chase the dream of wealth," sighed Remone.

"Another way the Great Mystery speaks to me is through my dreams. I had a dream four winters ago. In my vision, I sat on a mountaintop in only my loin cloth while snow fell about me. The snow fell so hard that it covered me completely. I looked at my hand and saw that it had turned blue from the cold. The people of the village suffered greatly as the snow continued. We had not made provisions for such a severe winter. I saw many animals of the plains frozen by the storm."

"So what did your dream mean?" asked Remone.

"An early winter would come and catch us unaware unless we prepared. We hunted for deer and buffalo, dried and cured the meat, and set it aside for the winter. We also saved wood and placed it where it could be easily found."

"Did the storm come?"

"Our winter count shows that this was one of the earliest and worst snowstorms that the Sioux have suffered through, but we survived because we were ready!" the shaman answered, lifting his hands to the sky. "The Great Spirit loves us and sent me a warning."

"I wish I could have dreams that would give me direction in my life," said Remone.

"I think you do. The next time you dream, try to remember it and tell me what you saw. Talk to the Great Spirit. The answers will come to you through the small voice within."

23

Sun Dance/Kangee

THE FIRE HAD BURNED LOW, and the moon had waned in the sky as the shaman and Pinchot sat sharing the pipe and talking with Remone. The rest of the village slept as their talk turned to the Sun Dance ritual and preparing Remone for the trials he must endure as a part of it. Remone had many questions.

"Why is it necessary for me to give blood to Wakan Tanka? What purpose does it serve?" asked Remone.

"It is to purify your body and spirit," said Pinchot. "You must be purified to commune with the Great Spirit."

"But I thought I had already been purified by going on my vision quest."

"Your vision quest and being part of the Sun Dance celebration are two different things. You were given a gift of blood, and blood is what you must spill back to Wakan Tanka," said Pinchot.

"But how was I given blood?" asked Remone.

"In birth, you were given life and the blood beating like a war drum through your body," said the shaman. "In time, we will return the gift that was loaned to us by the Great Mystery. But now you must meet him face-to-face, make a pact with him, and thank him for making you Sioux. In this way, you will be able to ask him for help when you need him. Blood giving is to honor Wakan Tanka, and the pact must be sealed with blood to be real."

"Is there no other way? Is this really what the Great Spirit wants?"

"Through his doubts, man tests the Great Mystery. When we ask for the Great Spirit to prove something, we are testing him," said Pinchot.

"But isn't it only fair for him to provide proof of his will?" asked Remone.

"No, Remone, man's character must be tested as he grows in this world, but it is not for man to test the Great Spirit," explained the shaman.

"How would one test God?" asked Remone.

"There are many ways that man unknowingly tests the Great Spirit," answered the shaman. "Listen to the story of Kangee. He was a huge seven-foot-tall brave, known for having a violent temper. In a skirmish with the blue coats, Kangee killed three men by himself. He leaped from his horse with the fury of a madman and struck them down with his tomahawk. Then he scalped them and took trophies. The medals the blue coats wore looked like a great prize, so he took all he could find. This was forbidden, but he did not hide the decorations he took."

"Many believed they would be cursed by taking the White man's belongings into their homes. The shamans had spoken against it," said Returns Again. "But many could not resist the White man's clothes and medals. With blood on his hands, Kangee removed the medals and emblems from the soldier's collars. Then he took all the coins from their pockets and drove holes through them. Then he made a rope of hair from the scalps he had taken, stringing the medals and coins together. Defiantly he wore his horrific necklace for all to see.

"'A great sign of your valor in battle,' one of the braves said to Kangee. 'You are truly to be our leader,' another one of the braves said in awe. But others expressed themselves, 'No, Kangee, do not tempt fate. Do not go against the laws of our people.' Still, Kangee's collection grew. The taking of hats or the White man's guns were one thing, but trophies such as scalps might give the braves power over the Whites in the afterworld. But the taking of coins and medals was an act of greed.

"Kangee went into the mountains," the shaman continued, "to the place where the Sioux practiced their sacred rituals. This was considered holy ground. A temple without walls that Wakan Tanka had given the Sioux. Here Kangee practiced the rite of blood sacrifice, puncturing himself repeatedly as an offering to the Great Spirit. But the Great Spirit rejected Kangee's attempt to commune with him.

"The Great Spirit changed himself into a storm cloud—dark, foreboding, and full of anger—he charged in from the west, speaking in a voice that made the mountains shake. 'Kangee!' shouted the Great Spirit with a voice of thunder. 'I see you have brought the bloody scalps of your enemies into my sacred place!'

"Proudly he stood when he should have kneeled," the shaman said. "The Great Spirit acted on Kangee's sacrilege. The judgment was clear. The lightning bolt struck straight into Kangee's chest where the metals were held by the string of scalps. On his charred black body, the medals and coins had burned into his skin. The impressions could be clearly seen.

"Kangee violated the sacred place by bringing his trophies of the Whites into it. What was meant as a place to worship Wakan Tanka was tainted by his actions. Kangee was punished for it," the shaman explained. "It was as if he dared the Great Spirit to do something. And the Great Spirit had answered."

Remone knew the metal had served as a conductor for the lightning to strike. Like a lightning rod, the metal that hung from his neck attracted the bolt that fried his chest and ended his life. But Remone said nothing to the shaman. He thought he was correct. Kangee put God to the test and lost.

24

T HE DAWN CAME AND THE tribe awoke to a warm summer day. The spring rains had stopped, so the ground was dry. Remone filled his quiver with arrows and went to get Little Wing.

Pinchot met him. "I have been waiting for this time of the year. Now the weather is good for what I wanted to show you."

"I am ready to do my part for the tribe," said Remone as he held up his bow. "I have been practicing my skill with the arrow."

"Today we will hunt but not to feed the tribe. Today we will search for the home of the Sioux," said Pinchot. "I will show you where we came from."

Pinchot led Remone into the Black Hills high above their village on the river. "Here we will find the cave known as Sacred Breath," said Pinchot as they continued their ascent.

Stopping for water at a mountain spring, Pinchot and Remone rested their horses.

"Look, the teepees in the valley look like little rows of hay stacked for the harvest," said Remone as he shaded his eyes.

"Smell the wood lilies," said Pinchot. "They only bloom at this time of the year."

On they rode as hawks perched like sentinels watching from the ponderosa pines called out to them as they passed.

"I think this is the place," said Pinchot as they came to a bend in the trail, where a large white boulder rose from the ground.

"Wait here and see if I can find it," said Pinchot as he slid down from his horse.

Remone watched as Pinchot pulled back the underbrush. "Where is it?" Pinchot said to himself as he stood and used his hand to check his alignment with the large white rock. He disappeared into the brush.

"This must be a pretty small hole?" said Remone over the sound of Pinchot breaking branches.

"Just big enough for us to fit into," answered Pinchot. "Oh, here it is," Pinchot said as he pulled back an indigo bush.

Remone tied Little Wing's reins to a tree and came to look. A hole the size of a man's torso lay behind the bush. "That is a really small entrance," said Remone.

"Get closer and feel the wind," said Pinchot.

As Remone stooped down to look in the opening, his hair blew back. "It is like a storm coming out of the cave," exclaimed Remone. "But it is a warm wind."

"Yes, the cave breathes hard," Pinchot agreed.

"I thought it was just legend," said Remone. "How did you find this cave?"

"We did not find this cave," said Pinchot. "It is where we the Sioux people came from. Its sacred breath gave us life. You should see it in the winter when it looks like smoke blowing out of the cave because of the warmth within her walls."

"You don't expect me to crawl into this tunnel, do you?" asked Remone.

"This is another one of the holiest places on earth for the Sioux, so we treat it with the reverence she deserves. We do not want it to be easy to find. Going down this passage is like crawling back into the womb of Mother Earth. A woman's body is holy, so see how this is done."

Pinchot stood up and looked up into the sky and slowly raised his outstretched palms in the air as if he was making an offering of himself. After several deep breaths, he called out, "Great Spirit, guide us as we seek to discover your mysteries and see your beauty."

Then Pinchot, on his elbows with his chest on the ground, squeezed his way into the tiny opening in the ground. He pushed a pouch containing torches in front of him. "Do not worry, Remone, the cave gets larger the farther you crawl down."

Remone looked in, and when he could not see Pinchot's legs anymore, he yelled into the cave, "Are you okay?"

There was no answer, so Remone apprehensively followed, crawling in just the way Pinchot had. Sliding on the moist, muddy floor of the cavern, he made his way down in total darkness, but he could hear Pinchot in front of him scraping his way down into Mother Earth's belly.

In the darkness, Remone's imagination played tricks on his mind. Please don't let me get stuck and die in this hole. He wanted to see light and awaken from what seemed like a nightmare. He wallowed through the tunnel as fast as he could. After what seemed like an eternity, he heard Pinchot striking a flint.

The room expanded in the light, reflecting off the millions of quartz crystals that covered the walls. Remone and Pinchot sat, spellbound by the beauty of the labyrinth.

Pinchot whispered as he pointed, "See how the room sparkles like stars in the night."

"It is like the treasure room of a king," said Remone.

"This cavern is endless. Our sacred stories tell of the Sioux coming from another world, traveling though this portal and into this space. Here they increased in number and strength."

"Sounds like a wormhole," said Remone.

"Maybe the wormhole of a really big worm," said Pinchot as he passed his pipe to Remone.

"Let's go into the next chamber," Pinchot said as he stood up and walked upright to an opening on his left. Remone followed him as he stooped down to clear the opening.

"This is called the honeycomb. See the empty hives that she fed our people with? The bees have long since gone from the cave. Their job was done when the Sioux emerged from their home here and into the light of day."

"How did the bees get in here?" asked Remone.

"The Great Mystery showed his purpose to the bees and guided them into the cave to feed our people while they were still in the womb."

"How do you keep from getting lost in here?"

Pinchot stood and stretched before he walked over to a wall. "See, here are markings to guide us. This is like a giant maze, but there are others who have gone before us. We will go this way. They were able to stand and walk into the next chamber as they continued to go down deeper into the depths of the earth." As they walked, Pinchot grabbed Remone's shoulder, "Look out, there is a steep drop here."

Remone inched closer to the precipice that dropped hundreds of feet down onto sharp rocks. They could hear water flowing from a river deep inside the cave.

"We will rest here," said Pinchot as he plopped down, dangling his feet over the edge. "Did you see the river below? This is the wet season, so you can hear the river over the voice of the cavern's wind. It takes a rising river to feed the land. All is sustained by her gift. This is the sacred water that feeds our people and all life above in the Black Hills. In the winter months, the cavern is like an old woman dried and cracking, but spring brings rebirth."

"It is like a world within a world," said Remone.

Sitting on the precipice was like sitting on a mountaintop looking down on the valley below. The temperature was the same summer or winter. Protected from the rain and freezing cold, Remone could see why they called it home. There was a kind of magic at work in its depths. Maybe it was the flickering of the small torch Pinchot carried, but Remone started to see things in the shadows. There was a presence that made him feel small. He could understand the religious reverence the Sioux felt.

"What is this room called?" asked Remone.

"This room is called Mother's Milk. Look up and tell me what you see."

Remone looked up and realized he had been fixated on the wonders below, but the ceiling rose up hundreds of feet above them. Stalactites hung by the thousands, dangling from the ceiling. They were still growing as they dripped white water with limestone in it.

"It does look like milk dripping to the floor," said Remone with a whisper.

"This shelter brings life to what lives within these walls and above us in the soil of the Black Hills. You are witness to one of the great secrets of the Sioux."

As they rode away from the great cavern, Remone felt a sense of wonder. Being in the dark cave had been a religious experience for him; emerging from the cave, he squinted his eyes to see for the first time.

The duo rode for miles down from the mountains. The plains spread out before them, but as they reached the crest of the hill, Pinchot's horse neighed and kicked his front feet into the air. For as far as they could see, dead buffalo lay rotting on the ground. Vultures circled in the sky and pecked at the remains on the ground. Pinchot was speechless and then yelled, "No!" and charged down to the carnage. Remone followed on a skittish Little Wing.

Pinchot jumped from his horse and ran to kneel beside one of the big bulls. The buffalo had been skinned, but all the meat was left to spoil. Flies buzzed and laid their eggs in the holes oozing blood from the buffalo's decaying bodies. The stench of dead flesh reached Remone's nose as he dropped to his knees and emptied his stomach.

"I see the hand of the White man in this," said Pinchot as he felt the bullet hole with his finger.

The whole scene was too much for Remone to bear. "Who does this? This meat could have fed our tribe for the whole winter."

"Only fools," said Pinchot. "Only the Whites could do this."

25

A S THEY SAT AROUND THE fire that night, the shaman said to Remone. "We would like you to take a vow to participate in the Sun Dance. When the sun is at its highest in the sky, you must stare into it as if into the eyes of the Great Mystery and offer up your blood in appreciation of the life you have been given."

"The shaman will be your guide just as he was for your vision quest," said Pinchot.

"A sacrifice is the offering of something precious given for a cause. Your cause is to show your gratitude," said the shaman.

"All right, I will do it," said Remone.

Pinchot grabbed his shoulder. "Good, we will proclaim it to the tribe."

Remone realized this was his chance to show Black Wolf and his followers what he was made of. No, he would not falter. He would give up his blood.

Later that night, as he slept in his teepee, Remone's dreams turned to the ritual to come. In his dream, he saw the young maiden leading them to the tree they had chosen. She looked like a virgin. She looked angelic. She pointed to the tree and back to Remone, choosing him for the sacrifice. He saw the sun in the sky and the pole being raised.

Remone awoke from his dream. He crawled from his teepee, inhaling the cool night air. He felt at peace within himself. It flowed through his body and eased his mind. *Yes, I am ready to do this. I am ready to offer myself up.*

26

THE SUMMER SUN SMILED DOWN on the Sioux village on the
Cheyenne River. Life in the village was never more exciting
than when the tribe prepared for the Sun Dance ritual. All the
other tribes migrated to celebrate the summer equinox. The village
had already swollen in size. Old friends who had not seen each other
for a year were reunited. Each tribe camped in their own circle, with
all tribes together forming a larger circle.

The Shaman Returns Again sat at the communal fire surrounded
by shamans from the surrounding Sioux tribes. Sees through the Mist
from the Rosebud tribe sat next to Behind the Sun from the Standing
Rock tribe. The old Shaman Akomat from the Pine Ridge tribe sat
with his protégé, a much younger shaman, Icaro.

The younger, less experienced apprentice sat silent as Akomat
introduced him to the other shamans. "Icaro has the gift of the magic
song. He has shown great promise in learning the skills of healing as
I have taught him. The village has benefited greatly from his ability
to find answers from the spirit world of our ancestors."

"Has he learned the ways of talking to the Great Mystery's emissaries of the animal kingdom?" the Shaman Returns Again asked.
"Has he found the path to knowing other men's minds or visions of
the future?"

"These powers may need to be honed under a master," Akomat
answered. "Some time under your instruction, Returns Again would
lead him to be a great shaman."

"I am here for him and would welcome the help of one younger
and eager to learn," answered Returns Again. "What say you, Icaro?"

"Much have I learned from my teacher, Akomat. But from my
childhood, all have heard the name Returns Again."

"And these things that have been said were true?" The shaman laughed. "Did they not tell you the Shaman Returns Again is old and often falls asleep at the council fire?"

"These things we have heard in secret," Icaro replied. "But I will help nudge you when you nap."

"Stay with the Cheyenne tribe when the festival ends," Returns Again said. "I will take you to see the great medicine wheel."

The women of the tribe hurried to finish their quillworks. The artwork portrayed the different events in their lives. Each hoped that their masterpiece would be judged the winner.

The Standing Rock tribe had completed a special gift for the great Chief Slow Bull. They planned to present him with a pendant that used native stones and beads. The artwork honored the Great Spirit's messenger, the bald eagle. The wings were made of turquoise with beads forming the eyes and chest of the great bird.

Remone and Pinchot watched as Chatan, Kiowa, and Tusca prepared themselves for the archery contest.

"Last year, Okatee from the Rosebud tribe beat me using the bow," Tusca said. "But I have been practicing." He let an arrow fly. It hit the buffalo hide target just to the right of the bull's-eye.

"Here it is all in the feathers," Kiowa said as he showed Chatan the work he had done on his quiver of arrows. "You have to make sure the feathers are straight. I have been using beaver oil on the feathers to make them stiffer." Kiowa demonstrated as he wet his fingers in the oil and pulled the feathers taunt.

"Look how much smaller your feathers are," Chatan said, smiling as he showed them his. "I got these from the hawk's nest when she was not looking. The bigger the feathers, the more control over the flight."

Kiowa and Tusca looked like they had been slapped in the face. "Where did you say the hawk built her nest?" Tusca asked.

"Oh, I am not sure I remember, it may have been a long way from here," teased Chatan.

Pinchot interrupted the threesome to ask, "What are the braves doing this morning?"

The three boys hesitated to answer. They looked at Pinchot, suspiciously awaiting to hear what task Pinchot might have for them so close to the time of the great festival.

"It has been asked of Chaska and me to be the ones to choose the tree for this year's Sun Dance ritual," said Pinchot. "But we will need the help of your young eyes in choosing the right cottonwood. Can you help us pick out the right tree?"

The three boys' eyes lit up. Picking out the tree for the celebration was usually an honor reserved for those braves who had earned the right in combat. They ran to their teepees and put their bow and arrows away.

They met Pinchot and Chaska by the woods' edge and started their hike through the woods. Chaska was a much older brave and had been chosen to pick the tree because he had shown great valor in fighting the Crow. The boys were chosen to go to continue their learning of their tribe's traditions.

"When the Great Spirit measured the earth," said Pinchot, "he made sure he had saved the most holy of land for the Sioux. All who tread the earth walk upon sacred ground, but there are some places that are even more sacred."

"Like the medicine wheel," said Remone. "That is certainly one of the Sioux's most sacred of places."

"Yes, you have witnessed the wheel, it is one of the holiest of the gifts we have received. One of the most special trees to us is the cedar," Pinchot said, pointing to the ancient red cedar that rose over seventy feet into the air, towering above the other trees.

"How did it get so big?" asked Chatan.

"It has been alive for over a hundred years and known as the Tree of Life to our village," said Pinchot. "It is connected to all living things, but the circle of life has been broken. Let us pray for healing and the hoop will be complete again. See, the tree is sick. It will be whole when the world is whole again."

"How can you tell it is sick?" asked Tusca.

"See the needles that have fallen to the ground, honoring the tree that has held them within her grip for years. Without being connected, they wither and dry on the ground."

"I have heard that we burn cedar in our religious rites," said Kiowa. "Because it is the favorite of Wakinyan the Great Thunderbird."

"Yes, the smell of cedar is supposed to be pleasant to him," said Pinchot. "We also burn cedar and sage in our sweat lodge when performing the sacraments of purification."

The group continued farther into the woods until they came upon a meadow where a warm wind blew through the knee-high tallgrass. "It has warmed since morning," said Pinchot. "This water tastes good."

"I will be ready for a swim when we return to the village," said Kiowa.

"Me too," said Chatan, "after my chores are done."

"Look, the cottonwood grove," Chaska said as they walked closer to the trees that grew along the stream.

"They look much the same," Chatan said as they stood beneath them.

"That is why we brought you," Pinchot said. "Show us one you find worthy for us to mark for the festival. Remember, we do not want the tallest or widest or heaviest, since we have to carry it a long way back to the village. A good one must be young and green, not too old so it can hold the worshipper up to the sun."

"And straight, the tree must be straight," said Chaska.

After walking among the trees, Tusca looked up, admiring the tree above him. "How about this one," said Tusca.

"This looks good," said Pinchot. "What do you think, Chaska?"

"Tusca has chosen a fine tree," said Chaska. "It looks young and strong. It will point the way to the sun."

"I will mark it so it will be easy to find," said Pinchot. He took out a red deerskin and tied it around the trunk of the tree. "This will make it easier to find when we return."

27

"CHATAN, LET'S GO SWIMMING," SAID Tusca.

"I cannot go until my chores are done," answered Chatan. "I still have to gather firewood."

"We will help," said Tusca, looking at Kiowa, who nodded his head. "This is the perfect day for our new swimming hole."

The three friends made their way down the path gathering wood. Only one of the chores the young braves performed for the tribe. It was also an opportunity for distraction. Teenagers set for mischief.

Each load of wood took them closer and closer to the riverside and their swimming hole.

"Look what the braves left us." Tusca pointed to the fishing poles lying next to a tree.

"Oh, we need to leave those," Chatan, always the cautious one, said. "They will be back to get them in a minute."

"The trout are biting, don't be such a squaw, Chatan," said Kiowa, taunting him as he dropped the wood he was carrying and picked up one of the poles.

"These belong to someone," said Chatan.

"Look! There are three poles!" said Tusca. "One for each of us. Fishing has been destined."

Tusca took a pole and crashed through the brush in the direction of the river. Kiowa was close behind. A reluctant Chatan carried the last pole.

The summer sun shone down on them as they reveled in their youth, running down the hill looking for an adventure.

"I wish I had a basket to put all the trout in...," Tusca said, but just before he finished, he crouched to his knees and said, "Shhhh, do you hear that?"

The three boys huddled in the brush and listened. The faint sound of laughter could be heard over the sound of the river. The boy's eyes widened as Tusca pointed toward the sound, and they crawled Sioux-style through the bushes, clothed only in their loincloths.

Quietly, they reached the bank of the river where they could see the young Indian maidens splashing below in the water. The girls giggled as they saw how much their breasts had grown over the winter. Just below on a sandbar, one girl lay naked on a blanket, warming herself in the sun.

The young braves inched closer to the source of their young girl fantasies. Their prize was so close at hand. It was more than curiosity that drove them wild. How lucky could they be to find the girl's favorite swimming spot and to find their fathers' fishing poles unattended.

Suddenly, they were there! One parent grabbed Tusca by his ear and pulled him up to his feet. "What are you doing spying on my daughter?" he yelled.

"I'm sorry," Tusca cried as he ran away.

Another father grabbed Kiowa and kicked him in the ass, sending him running as fast as he could away from the angry fathers. Chatan was already down the path and hiding from the annoyed fathers.

Later, the three joined each other on the trail back to the village. "What I saw made me thank the Great Spirit for giving me life," said Tusca as he laughed.

I saw Chatan's loincloth sprouting a tree," said Kiowa.

"Here we must pick up the wood," said Chatan. "We have to bring something back to burn on the village fire."

Later, around the campfire, the parents of the girls complained about the boys' visit to their private swimming hole. "Now we will have to find a new place to swim," said one of the fathers.

"We should talk to the tribal council," said another.

"Let's talk to Pinchot," said another. "He knows the boys and has been active in their instruction."

"He is like a teacher to the boys."

"That is a good idea," they all agreed. "He will know what to do."

Pinchot was summoned to the fire circle. He tried hard not to laugh at the exploits of his young friends. "I recommend their punishment be a week of shoveling out dung from the horse stalls," said Pinchot. "It is a job that needs doing and will fill their idle hands. I will let them know this is the parents' decision."

Pinchot confronted the three and told them what their punishment would be.

"That is not fair," Tusca complained. "I feel as if I have already been punished after crawling through the poison ivy." He pointed to his legs and private parts where the familiar rash was visible.

Both Chatan and Kiowa shook their heads in agreement. "We did not go out to spy on the girls but happened upon them accidentally," said Kiowa.

"But you knew you should leave and did not," said Pinchot. "I have parlayed with the parents, and this is an acceptable punishment."

Shamed, the boys nodded their heads in acceptance of Pinchot's judgment.

28

REMONE RETURNED TO THE SWEAT lodge to prepare himself for the Sun Dance ritual. He would purify himself for four days to be pure enough to commune with Wakan Tanka—pure enough to hear his message. Remone had only water to drink. His impaling to the glory of the sun would mark his passing from being White to becoming a member of the Sioux tribe.

The ceremony began at dawn, when the young girl who had been chosen because of her purity followed them back to the tree. She looked just as Remone had imagined her in his dream. The woods were beautiful at this time of day. The sunlight fell in beams on the trees, giving them a golden hue that shined like honey. It added a sacredness to the morning and the celebration. "This is the tree that will point the way to the sun and the Great Spirit," the maiden said as she stood under its branches, looking up.

With a shout, the tribes cut the tree down. The braves trimmed the cottonwood, threw ropes over the branches, and, led by the chosen maiden, carried it reverently back to the village.

All seven Sioux tribes worked to build the roof in the shape of a circle. The Shaman Returns Again blessed the house. "To you, O Great Spirit, we dedicate this as your holy place! May it serve to honor you!"

The tribes gathered for the raising of the center pole. All the virgins in the camp came and touched the pole to proclaim their purity. The shamans chanted prayers while the braves stood by waiting for the signal. Then the whole village shouted, "Hiyo! Hoe!" And the pole yanked by the braves leapt into the air and settled firmly in the space prepared for it.

The drums began beating out a rhythm that the singing women danced to. They rose on the heels of their feet up and down as they circled the pole, moving in a continuous circle to celebrate the cycle of life. They vowed to dance throughout the whole ceremony with no food or water except for the rainwater the Great Spirit might bless them with during the ritual.

Fear gripped Remone as he crawled from the sweat lodge to join the celebration apprehensively. The crowd that circled the Sun lodge cheered for him. Wearing only his loincloth, he looked weak from his lack of food and loss of weight. The shaman led the celebrants in a prayer for healing, for the circle of life to continue, and for the hoop to be restored. Then the shaman and other participants took the ceremonial paint and colored Remone's face with stripes of red and black. He tried not to wince from the pain when they took the buffalo bones and pierced his chest. The shaman worked hard to get the bones deep enough into his flesh to hold him suspended for the length of the celebration. Then the chosen braves pulled Remone to the roof where he hung from the center pole to prove to all his manhood. All day he hung from the roof of the lodge. Women continued to dance in the ring around Remone while braves blew tuneless music on their eagle bone whistles; the piercing sound filled the holy space, building up the excitement to the climax of the ritual.

Spinning slowly in the air, Remone had his vision. He was riding his white mustang faster and faster up a trail that grew thinner and thinner until it was just a ribbon of light that gave him a path he could ride. He could see Wakan Tanka's smiling face in the sun, greeting him as he galloped into the fiery orb.

But he blacked out before he hit the sun before the bison bones tore through his flesh and the leather tongs sprung lose. He fell from the roof to the floor where Pinchot and the shaman caught him. Pinchot covered him with a blanket as the blood poured from his body.

"The bloody blanket for Wakan Tanka," Pinchot proclaimed proudly.

Remone with his sacrifice had earned his place in the tribe and settled his debt to the Great Spirit.

29

IME IS WAKAN TANKA'S THRESHING room floor.

The shaman took the young braves out to watch the corn harvest, many of them resented being led to observe what they considered to be the work of the women of the tribe.

"See how in the harvesting of the corn the ears are spread out in the sun to dry. Then when the corn has dried, the corn can easily be separated from the husk. It is necessary to separate the shuck from the corn's husk. It is the same way the Great Spirit harvests men," said the shaman.

"What becomes of the husks?" asked Chatan.

"They are thrown into the harvest fire," Tusca answered.

"Yes, as it has no purpose left, it is burned. The Great Spirit could make all of us live forever and be invincible, but this does not serve his purpose," said the shaman.

The braves watched as the women of the tribe applied their next skill passed down from generation to generation of mothers teaching daughters how to grind the corn. They worked the maize through a series of bins holding various-sized stones—from coarse larger stones to bins with finer stones—until they had a smooth flour they could easily store and cook with.

"Much is to be learned," said the shaman. "In the same way the women grind the corn, the Great Mystery takes a man and grinds him down to make him into something new. The troubles of this life tear away at a man like the women kneading the corn against the stone."

The braves nodded in affirmation of the shaman's words as they saw it with their own young eyes.

"The limitations of time force us to act now and not to waste the day for it is not unlimited. This is what gives our lives the most meaning and makes the days we do have the most precious to us," said the shaman. "Time is what the Great Mystery imposes on us to determine our worthiness to continue."

30

THE SHAMAN RETURNS AGAIN was a mystic, mysterious, having magical abilities he could use to heal. But did he also possess psychic powers? Or was his greater knowledge the result of emissaries such as the birds, owls, eagles, and other animals that carried the Great Mystery's messages to his servant?

The group of young braves were joined by Icaro walking through the woods along a path as the Shaman Returns Again showed them the different herbs that were good for healing. "Here is the Seneca snakeroot. This is good for making a poultice when one has been bitten by a spider or snake. All should carry some of this in their shot pouch."

He reached into the soil and pulled it up by the roots and passed it on to his students. "See the white flowers on the top and the vein on the back of the leaf. This is how you will recognize it from the other plants."

Separating the leaves from the root, the shaman explained, "This is the root one would chew on, eating some and taking the remainder to place on the bite to draw out the poison."

He demonstrated this as he removed the softened root from his mouth and placed it on an imaginary bite on his leg.

"And here is the hyssop plant." The shaman pointed to the green stems growing a foot tall in the meadow where the bright summer sunlight helped in their growth. Honeybees flew from blossom to blossom, pleasantly buzzing as they pollinated the purple flowers. "This is what one would use on cuts and bruises, smell the sweet fragrance."

As they continued walking up the sunlit trail, birds celebrated the beauty of the day in song as they flew through the treetops, stopping to rest on the branches and sing. The shaman continued his teaching as they slowly ascended the mountain. He called upon the young braves to think by asking them questions. He often chose this method to teach rather than telling them what to believe. "When you fast and go into the wilderness, where do you find yourself?"

"Are you talking about the wilderness of nature or into the wilderness of one's soul?" Pinchot asked philosophically.

"When you go into the Great Silence, what do you hear?" the shaman asked his group of students eager for knowledge.

"How can one hear the silence?" Remone asked in a weary voice.

"Still the voices in your head that are like a hundred barking dogs until the one and only voice you hear is that of silence. Do you listen to your own desires plotting to obtain more possessions or to the voice Wakan Tanka directing your feet to the path he has chosen for you?"

"But what are the ways one can enjoy soul growth, teacher?" Kiowa asked the shaman.

"Those who have suffered in the flesh can relate to others' suffering," the shaman answered. "We feel compassion for others if we have felt the same pain."

"I want more power to be able to read others' minds," said Chenoa.

"Become more spiritual and other powers will follow," the shaman said. "Draw close to the Great Mystery and the powers of prophecy to see into men's hearts, and what they are thinking will follow. But one should come before the other."

"How is a man transformed not just on the outside but down to his core, from the inside out?" the shaman asked his students. "The words I speak may cause a stirring in your heart, but what changes a man so you can see it in his actions?"

The shaman could see Remone struggling with his progress. "Let me tell you the story of Tesca Hoh. He grew up a happy child in his Sioux village, but he was small in stature and slight of frame. As he grew, some of the other braves teased him for being what they thought was feminine and overly sensitive. In despair, he held his tears and fled into the woods, traveling deep into the Black Hills, determined not to return to the Sioux village even if it meant his dying in the forest unsung and alone.

"As night began to fall, he looked in his pack and found the corn cakes he had taken from his mother's vessels of food. His stomach growled, and he regretted only taking two from her cache. Slowly he became aware of a figure standing just beyond the light of his fire. Startled, he sat completely still as his eyes adjusted to the light.

"An aged Indian approached his fire, his long white hair draping down past his shoulders. His face was withered with dark lines framing his pale tired eyes. As he panted for breath, Tesca felt compassion as he jumped to his feet and ran to help the old man. 'Here let me help you. Sit here and warm yourself by the fire.'

"'I have been lost in the hills,' the old man explained. 'Might you have anything to eat?' Sighing, Tesca Hoh reached inside his pack and said, 'Just my mother's corn cakes,' as he handed one to the old man. He reached back into the bag and took the only remaining cake and broke off a piece for himself. The old man devoured the corn cake, and it looked like he was going to pass out.

"Stirring the fire, Tesca looked back at the old man and was shocked to see him standing transformed with new life shining in his eyes. 'I am Oyate, thank you for sharing with me when you have so little to share.' Tesca began to realize that he was dealing with a holy man. 'We have seen your struggles,' his visitor said. 'Come with me deeper into the Black Hills, and we will transform Tesca Hoh.' Speechless but shaking his head affirmatively, Tesca agreed to go with him.

"Oyate reached for a pouch around his belt and poured a purple powder out into the palm of his hand and yelled an incantation, 'Take us into the heart of Paha Sapa to nourish Tesca Hoh!' He threw the powder into the fire, sending up a cloud of smoke. When the smoke cleared, they found they had been transported into a cave deep beneath the Black Hills. They found themselves not alone but in the company of other ancient Indians, and they began to talk amongst themselves as if Tesca Hoh was not even there. Oyate turned back to Tesca Hoh and said, 'Your transformation begins in the morning. Tonight, we feast!' He led Tesca Hoh to a hall within the cave where a table lay covered with food, waiting to be eaten.

"In the morning, Oyate took Tesca Hoh down into the valley where water tumbled over stones that lay in the creek bed. Oyate pointed with his staff to the stones. 'These must be moved. Up to the top of the mountain.' 'B-B-But that's not possible,' Tesca Hoh stuttered with a laugh. 'How can I, one little brave, move these stones up this mountain?' 'Begin with this one.' Oyate tapped his staff against a boulder. It was round and weighed almost a hundred pounds. 'But how?' asked Tesca. 'Roll it up the path.' Oyate pointed to a small winding path that meandered up the mountain. Oyate turned and walked away, leaving Tesca Hoh to the task.

"The sun began to set as a weary Tesca Hoh stumbled back to the cave. Oyate asked the young brave, 'How many stones did you move?' 'How many? Only the one,' Tesca Hoh answered. 'Good! You have earned your evening meal, go and eat.' A very tired Tesca ate his fill and fell asleep.

"In his dreams, he flew over the valley where he played as a child. He saw his mother cooking buffalo stew in the cooking pots over the fire. He could smell the pleasant aroma as he saw his friends retiring from their chores to sit by the communal fire. They were joking and having fun together as they sharpened their arrowheads and worked on their bow and arrows.

"In the morning, Tesca awoke to a staff prodding him to get up. 'Time to begin your work.' said Oyate. 'Here this stone needs to go up the mountain today.' Oyate tapped his staff on an even larger boulder. Then he turned around and walked away.

"For ten new moons, Tesca Hoh rolled boulders up to the mountaintop. The largest rocks that would roll were gone from the creek bed. But Tesca's temper raged hot as he questioned why he had been brought from the comfort of his village to suffer in such a way in the wilderness. He forgot the torment of his peers and why he had escaped into the Black Hills.

"Oyate pointed to the largest boulders. 'These, too, need to make the trip to the mountaintop.' said Oyate. Tesca Hoh gave Oyate an incredulous look. 'But how is this to be done?' asked Tesca. 'These rocks are not round and will not roll.' Oyate presented Tesca with a large hammer. It was a stone tied with rawhide to a wooden pole three feet long. 'You will break them into smaller stones. You will carry the broken pieces to the top.'

"After Tesca Hoh had smashed these stones down to a smaller size, Oyate returned with a large basket fashioned with shoulder straps so that it could be thrown over one's back. With a look of exasperation, Tesca Hoh could hold back no longer. 'What purpose does this serve? Why have you brought me here to torment me?' With patience, Oyate said, 'When we met, you agreed to come with me and asked not how we would transform you. You have followed our discipline well and are much changed.'

"Picking up a rock, Oyate turned it over in the palm of his hand, examining it. 'Stones like these are much like people, the hardest blows soften them the most, breaking down their hearts of stone. Even the song of the river trickling over the stones with enough time makes them smooth and polished.'

"The elders used the stones to build a medicine wheel to mark the changing of the seasons. The hoop represented the never-ending cycle of life, with no beginning and no end. The cross inside the wheel pointed to the four winds. Objects like eagle feathers were placed in the center of the wheel, a sign of the Great Spirit's power over all things. The center used the rocks Tesca had crushed to make the surface smooth and easy to stand upon. Spokes were formed by rows of lager rocks. The boulders gave the circle a barrier where participants could sit while they directed rituals to heal the sick and celebrate the passing of time.

"The choice of the location on the mountaintop was of great significance. It was important that the wheel be seen from above. Since the medicine wheel was used for healing. It needed to be visible to the Great Spirit. Great care was taken to study the alignment of the stars so they could mark the longest day of the year within the wheel. The Sioux used the medicine wheel to illustrate their view of the galaxy. Functioning as a calendar for the Sioux, it was also to be a site for celebration and dancing to honor the Great Spirit.

"Still, Tesca felt he had been used. He yearned to return to his tribe. Oyate acknowledged his discontent. 'It is time for you to return to your people. Come up the hill with me one last time.' As they reached the top, Oyate explained many things to the young brave. 'When you came to us, you were small and slight of frame, but as the stones you moved grew larger, so did Tesca. As the wheel was built, so was your frame. Now you are a changed man. Know that you are not changed in body only but inside as well. Sometimes what Wakan Tanka gives us as adversity is intended to make us grow spiritually. Some suffer great illness to take themselves to where you are today. Through your trials, your body has grown stronger, now you must use your lesson to make your soul stronger too. It is time for you to return home.' The two embraced, and Oyate threw a handful of white powder into the air above them. When Tesca Hoh breathed it in, he fell into a deep sleep.

"Tesca Hoh awoke to the sound of the river where he played as a child. He followed the path where he had hunted as a boy back to his village, easily finding his way back home. As he approached the clearing and saw the teepees, he became excited and began to run. His mother was kneading corn and saw him as he approached. She leaped up with excitement. 'My son has returned to me!'

"While they embraced, the whole village began to gather around them. In whispers, his peers expressed astonishment at how Tesca had changed. Heavier and covered in muscles, none of them made fun of him anymore because he had become bigger than any of them. What his peers could not see were the changes Tesca Hoh had undergone inside. In flexing his strength of will to overcome his challenge, he had stretched his mind. In this way, he had grown in ways that even he himself did not yet understand.

"The Great Spirit works with men's hearts much in the way a maiden works with clay to form pots and vessels to hold water. In what way will the problems you are challenged with today help you to grow?" the shaman asked the braves as he began to walk again, with them following in step as they continued to explore the hidden treasures of nature.

31

THE WOMEN OF THE VILLAGE were cooking soup again as they stirred their kettles over the fire. Adding field grass to the water, they stretched their food supply so all could eat.

"This soup is so thin," said Tusca. "Is there no meat in it?"

"Shhhh," said Pinchot, holding his finger to his lips. "Be grateful for what you have." Then he tasted the soup for himself and walked away from the fire to hide his face as he spit out the flavored water.

"Let us see if we can add anything to this stew," Pinchot said quietly to Remone so that no one else would hear.

Remone followed Pinchot to the large teepee where food was stored. Seeing the empty pots was Pinchot's call to action.

Rainy weather had made it hard to hunt, and the tribe's supply of food was running low. They had already preserved buffalo meat by cutting it into lean strips and drying it in the sun, but the women had hidden it away for the winter months, when it would be needed the most. What they needed now was another source of sustenance for their immediate needs.

A break in the rain gave Pinchot an opportunity to lead his group of young braves out on a foggy morning to hunt.

"Today we will practice trapping our food," said Pinchot. "In these heavy rains, the animals have sought shelter just as we have done. But they, too, are becoming hungry, and we will use that to catch them. How many of you have ever used a snare?"

"My father has shown me how this is done," said Kiowa.

"Show us what you have learned."

"A snare is not for big game but something more the size of a bird or a rabbit. You take a vine and tie it to a young sapling." Kiowa demonstrated by tying a vine to a tree branch. "Fasten it to the ground. Make the vine into a loop tied as a noose. When the stick becomes dislodged, the noose tightens around the animal's leg as the sapling springs upright."

"Very good, Kiowa, you have learned much from your father. See that the noose is able to slide tighter with ease, or your prey will escape." Pinchot loosened the vine and demonstrated sliding it easily back and forth. The boys watched and nodded their acknowledgment of how it worked.

"Always be ready to make changes until your trap works. Did anyone bring the bait to attract a bird?" Pinchot asked.

The braves looked embarrassed at their lack of preparation as they stared back at Pinchot with blank faces.

"Let us see what we have here," Pinchot said as he pulled a pouch from his belt. "How about a little corn to catch a bird for dinner?" he said as he sprinkled some on the ground inside the loop of the snare.

"I have seen others use fish," said Tusca.

"Fish would work well, but I have none," said Pinchot. "One might even catch a bigger bird with fish. Now let us think, how many birds will we have to catch to feed the tribe?"

"We will have to set more traps," said Kiowa. "I would eat more than one quail by myself."

"Or we may need to have another plan to feed the whole village. Never be afraid to change your plan to achieve a different outcome," said Pinchot to the group. "Let us think about what would feed the most of us."

"What if we were to build a deadfall?" Tusca said to Pinchot.

"Have you ever built one of those?" asked Pinchot.

"I have worked on one. We used a heavy log tied to a tree by vines."

"What were you trying to kill?"

"Maybe a bear, I am not sure," Tusca answered.

"I have used the deadfall technique before," Pinchot said. "But it has proven to be more dangerous to me. The trigger to loosen the log and make it take flight often fails. I saw one brave get seriously hurt when the trap failed."

"I thought it was scary," Tusca agreed.

"Try as many ways to catch your food as you can and choose the one that suits you best," Pinchot said as he looked at each of the braves. "I am thinking we could use a pit. What do you think you could catch in a pit?"

"Maybe a bear?" said Tusca.

"A deer?" answered Chatan.

"All of those are good game to catch, as they would feed the village for many days. Let us work at building the pit and see what the Great Mystery provides," said Pinchot.

He handed the braves wood shovels and used a large bowl he had brought as bucket. The ground was soft from the rains, and they worked fast until they soon had a deep hole but not deep enough.

"It needs to be deeper," said Pinchot. "Deep enough so that you cannot crawl out."

"Then how do we get out?" asked Chatan.

"We will just use you for bait!" Pinchot laughed.

The pit was deep enough when it was Pinchot's height. He took a vine tied to a tree to pull himself out. "Good, now look for wood we can use as stakes, about as long my arm."

The braves brought back limbs for Pinchot's approval. "Make sure they are strong enough to hold our meal." Pinchot demonstrated by breaking one of the limbs with his hands. "This one is too weak, but they all work together just as we do to get it done."

Soon they had a pile of stakes that Pinchot sharpened. "This is enough, I will help you put them in place."

Spreading the stakes across the pit and pushing them deep enough into the mud to support them, Pinchot said, "Now this is the dangerous part. Take care that you do not fall back into the pit. I will put these in place, then you help pull me out."

"Our next task is to cover the hole, the branches need to be long enough, and we need to put them down where they cross each other for support. The trap should not fall until an animal steps on it." Pinchot demonstrated this by putting down the first branches with Remone's help. Then they added a layer of leaves until it was completely covered.

"How will we mark our trap so that we catch a bear or deer and not a Sioux brave?" asked Pinchot.

"I know," said Tusca. "We can mark it with two arrows and cross them like this."

"Now we must find something to use as bait. What will that be? What do we want to catch the most?" said Pinchot.

"I hunger for venison," said Chatan.

"I want to catch a bear," said Tusca.

"Let us think," said Pinchot. "What would these animals eat? A bear would eat corn or fish or any dead animal, but a deer is not going to eat of the flesh but more berries or tree bark. Sorry, Chatan, but I think deer is out unless one is clumsy and just falls into our pit. I think we need some fish to complete the trap. Let us see what we can pull from the river."

The braves fished the river, but it was Remone who yelled in a very White-sounding voice, "I got one!"

"My lessons in fishing have worked," said Pinchot. "A nice trout to place over our pit."

Pinchot carefully suspended the fish over the pit with a vine and lowered it down onto the leaves that covered the hole.

The rains started again as Pinchot looked up into the sky, saying, "Our work here is done. Tomorrow we will return to see what the Great Spirit has sent to us."

The next morning, Pinchot's group of braves was excited as they gathered around the village campfire.

"What will we have for dinner tonight?" mused Kiowa.

"I want bear," said Tusca. "My belly craves it. A bear would feed the whole village for weeks."

"Maybe it will be a coyote," said Kiowa. "They are good to eat."

"Good." Pinchot greeted the group. "You are all here. Are you ready to see what we have received?"

The group of young braves trudged through the muddy wet woods back to the place where they had placed the fish. It was very quiet. The only sound was their feet as the mud mushed beneath their moccasins. They could only see a short distance in the early morning fog that clung close to the ground. Their anticipation grew as they got closer. First, they came to their snare, but there was nothing in it, so they continued to the pit.

As they drew closer, Pinchot held out his arm. "Stop and listen. What is that sound?" The group stopped and listened.

A pathetic crying was coming from the direction of their trap. "What is that?" said Remone in a whisper.

"I do not know," said Pinchot. "Maybe a baby cat crying in the woods?"

In silence, they continued toward the sound. The young braves listened as they tried to imagine what they had caught.

Then as they drew closer, the sound grew more pathetic. "That sounds almost human," said Pinchot as he quickened his pace.

They could see a tear in the roof of the trap where the sticks had been. As they peered down into the pit, a pitiful voce called out, "Help me."

Pinchot looked at the markings on the skin of the young boy and immediately recognized him as being Crow, but his heart was moved with compassion. He slid into the trench with care and saw that three of the stakes had pierced the boy. He pulled his water pouch from over his back. "Here drink. My name is Pinchot. We will take care of you."

Pinchot looked up at the young braves who were just standing there, looking down into the hole. "Cut me some more vines and toss them down to me, I need to put a tourniquet on his arm and leg. We must get him out of this hole."

Remone crawled down into the hole. "Oh, he looks bad," said Remone in a low whisper.

"At least his wound in his stomach is not too deep. It just pierced his side," said Pinchot. "Hold this cloth on there and try to stop the blood. I will try to tie this vine around him."

"Do you think he will make it?" said Remone without thinking.

"We have to try!" said Pinchot. "Tusca, you and Chatan do not just stand there. Help us pull him out."

"But he is Crow," said Chatan.

"We will need to build a travois to carry him back to the village," said Pinchot. "Gather limbs."

But the braves were hesitant to help an enemy, even one that was their same age. Pinchot had to raise his voice to get any help as they begrudgingly responded to his orders.

Once they had him out of the pit, Remone took a closer look at the injured boy's stomach as Pinchot supervised building the gurney to carry him on.

"At least there are many of us to help," said Pinchot in a voice that all the boys could hear. "Each of us can help pull."

Upon reaching the village, Pinchot found the young braves were not the only ones who thought the Crow should not have been saved. Many of the men thought he should have been left to die. They questioned why he was so close to their village. Had he been spying on them?

Pinchot questioned him and found he was the son of one of the Crow chiefs.

"My name is Nyati. I am the son of Otakay. I was trying to prove myself worthy to my father. I seek to win the hand of a maiden, so I was trying to prove my courage before the tribe."

"I urge you to be silent in saying this to other Sioux, Nyati," said Pinchot.

But the young brave would not be silent.

The Sioux boys joked that since they had caught him, they should kill and eat him just as they would eat any other prey that had fallen into the pit.

The whole village agreed that there should be a meeting to decide what to do with Nyati. They talked of ransoming the young brave. If he was the chief's son, he would bring many fine horses.

He was led before the tribal council. "Why did you trespass onto Sioux land?" asked Chief Slow Bull to the wounded brave.

"To see how many horses were in your stables," answered Nyati proudly without fear of reprisal.

This angered many of the braves. "Why not kill Nyati? After all, he had already confessed to spying on them."

"Do we call ourselves a great race of people and take advantage of the weak or sick just because we are more powerful?" asked Pinchot.

"When I was a young brave," said Chief Slow Bull, "I learned the glory was not in killing just because you could. Many were the braves I struck in coup to show I could have killed, but I stayed my hand, my courage having been tested."

"But why should we not benefit from what we have found?" asked Black Wolf.

"Because there is no honor in it," answered Pinchot.

"Pinchot is right," said Chief Slow Bull. "We will show the boy mercy because we are Sioux, the great hunters of the plains. Untie him and you, Pinchot, will take him back to his people."

Pinchot had Nyati placed back on the travois and hitched it to Splitting Cloud. It was near nightfall when he approached the Crow village. Suddenly, he was surrounded by Crow warriors.

"What is a Sioux brave doing here? Do you think you can just ride into our village?" they growled at Pinchot.

"My business is not with you," answered Pinchot, "but with Chief Otakay, for this is his son, Nyati."

The braves looked on the gurney and let Pinchot pass. They showed him the way to the chief's teepee.

The chief came through the Crow village followed by more braves who took Pinchot from off his horse and held him captive. The chief knelt to look at his son. "Who has done this to you?"

"No one. I hurt myself," Nyati answered. "The Sioux brave Pinchot has brought me back. It was he that rescued me after my injuries."

"Then we will let him go." Otakay motioned to his braves as they released Pinchot, and he shook his arms free.

"Since you have come in peace, so will you return but not without a prize." The chief clapped his hands together, and another brave brought the chief's horse. "Let it not be said that Chief Otakay does not pay a debt even to a Sioux." He handed the reins to Pinchot.

It was later that night that a tired Sioux warrior rode back to the village on the Cheyenne River with another horse tied behind Splitting Cloud.

32

AT SUNRISE, ICARO AND THE Shaman Returns Again began their long hike up the mountaintop to the great medicine wheel. Many rode a horse to the top, but Returns Again wanted to use the trip to see what Icaro knew of the herbs and plants of the forest.

The blooms of large magenta petals unfurled in the late summer sun. "Do you recognize this plant? Has the Pine Ridge tribe been using these to cure ailments?" Returns Again asked as he tested the younger shaman.

Icaro stroked the blooms. "This is an echinacea plant. We make it into a tea. Here I have some in my pouch. It is good to have when the weather turns colder, and the breathing sickness spreads through the village."

"And this plant, have you seen it before?"

Icaro stooped down to pull some of the red flowers from the top of the green stalks. "This is the red yucca. We use it to treat old man ailments. For those whose bones ache from the cold. It can be eaten, but chewing a little to make a poultice to be placed on the skin also works very well."

"Very good," Returns Again answered. "Akomat has taught you well."

The two continued climbing until the morning sun had turned to late afternoon and Returns Again had grown weary in the heat. "Here let me catch my breath." Returns Again dropped his pack and wet his hair.

"My old bones ache from this trail."

"Should we stop here for the night?"

"No, let me rest a moment more," Returns Again answered as he wrapped a wet cloth around his head. "There is a clearing halfway up the mountain where we can camp."

As they stoked the fire and unrolled their bedrolls, Returns Again asked Icaro, "Have you practiced the art of the trance?"

"Some, but it is not something I have perfected," answered Icaro.

"Practice with me as the sun sets in the west."

Returns Again sat cross-legged with his eyes closed while the crickets sang good night to the sun. The final rays cast an indigo hue over the landscape as Icaro followed Returns Again's inaction, sitting perfectly still until the shaman began to speak in his ancient voice at a near whisper. "Let your gaze not be upon one thing. See like you are looking at nothing but seeing the whole world all at one time. Slow your mind until you feel a oneness. The silence you listen to will allow you to receive the message the Great Spirit has for you."

Transfixed on the fading light that the day was giving up, they listened to animal noises in the woods as some went to bed and others to hunt. The owl hooted his message of warning to the field mouse that it was prey for the badger.

Icaro broke the near silence. "What message does the Great Spirit bring to you?"

"He speaks to me through my stomach, which is growling loudly enough now to drown his voice," the shaman said as he rustled through his pack for food.

The pair arose early the next morning to continue their journey. A fog clouded their view of the valley below as they walked along the

ridge. While they stopped to rest, a large raven flew up to Returns Again and, cawing loudly, settled on his staff.

"This is Beltran," said Returns Again as he mimicked the raven's voice like they were carrying on a conversation. "We have been friends for many years," Returns Again said as he fed a handful of corn to the bird. "He brings me tidings from the spirit world."

"Here you feed him, Icaro."

As Icaro fed Beltran, he stroked his head. "Beltran is a good bird."

"He likes you," Returns Again said. "I hope you will be friends as long as we have been."

"How have you made Beltran talk to you?"

"No one makes Beltran do anything. He is an independent soul."

Beltran cawed loudly and nodded in agreement with the shaman's words.

"It has taken time to build trust and train my ears to understand what he says, but his speech is not so different than man's. I found Beltran as a baby chick without a mother and cared for him. That is why he is so loyal to me."

"Maybe I can do the same at Pine Ridge."

"Or stay here and learn from Beltran. It is just like learning any new language."

The duo continued climbing the summit with Returns Again leaning heavily on his staff to help push him along the way. The woods thinned, and the bald opened to expand the horizon. On a clear day like this one, the view was awe-inspiring.

"We are here," sighed a relieved shaman as he sat down on one of the boulders that encircled the wheel.

Icaro, the younger shaman, sighed but not from exhaustion. "This was worth the trip up. I have never seen a view like this before."

Returns Again told Icaro, "This wheel has been here as long as the Sioux people. Our descendants built it so long ago that no records date it. We will camp here tonight in the circle outside the ring. One can chart the changing in the seasons by looking at the night sky."

The weather was warm in the valley below, but here on the mountaintop it was cooler. The wind had nothing to block it as it blew in from the west, causing the fire to flicker with each gust. The shaman used his staff to point to the stars and the changing positions in the fall sky. "All the stars move except the Hunter's star. It stands still in the sky. The large spoke of the hoop points to it," the shaman explained. "This gives order to the universe. The wheel ties the earth and sky together."

"I can see the spirit path clearly from this height," Icaro mused. "It leads us to the home of our ancestors."

"Yes, on a clear night like this, it is beautiful to see."

In the morning, the pair made their descent back down the mountain. For two days, they hiked. As the pair rested on the trail, Icaro asked more questions of Returns Again to learn his skills. "What is your secret to knowing other men's thoughts and knowing the future?"

"It is not a secret. It is a practice. My many years of caring for others has allowed me to often know what they are thinking. Sometimes the dreams I have are visions that can be interpreted as lessons. All men should remember their dreams, for there are great messages within."

They stopped where the paths split—one way to Pine Ridge, the other the way back to Returns Again's home on the Cheyenne River.

"I have learned much from my time here in the Black Hills," said Icaro. "I enjoyed being with you and my Cheyenne brothers. But I feel the call of my kin at Pine Ridge."

"It is good. You will know when it is time for you to return." The shaman embraced Icaro and locked arms with him in a handshake. As Icaro began his journey back home, the shaman held his staff high, bidding farewell to his student.

33

What's that sound?
Rumbling across the plains,
somewhere in the distance,
but gaining speed.
Sounds like thunder,
but it's a thousand hoofs,
crashing through the fields
and stirring up the dust.
The leaves are falling,
so the time has come,
the Purple Buffalo is leading his herd
to a new grazing ground.

REMONE HAD LEARNED TO RESPECT the Sioux's conservation of their resources. To the Indians, their views of caring for their environment were inseparable from their deeply religious regard for Mother Earth. Generations had depended on the buffalo for food, clothing, and shelter, even down to the utensils used to eat with.

The divine teachings had been brought to them by the Sacred Buffalo Cow acting as a messenger from the Great Spirit. "Honor Mother Earth and Father Sky, for you live upon one and underneath the other." Nature was the Great Spirit's masterpiece, and he showed his handiwork across all creation. The buffalo was one of the greatest gifts the Great Spirit bestowed on the Sioux nation—a true sign of the love he felt for his people.

The tribes pursued the shrinking herds that were their source of food and spirituality. Chief Slow Bull spoke to his tribe and readied them for the chase. "When I was a young brave, the buffalo were so many they covered the plains in endless number. But now they are far fewer. The White man brought his iron horse to cover the land and tie down Mother Earth. With strands of steel, he tried to bind her. But our buffalo brothers ripped up the strands of steel from her body and freed her from the White man's grip. They scattered the steel rails and stomped them into the ground."

The Sioux tribe cheered, "To our buffalo brothers, long live the buffalo!"

"When the White man built fences to close off the open range," the chief cried out, "the buffalo protected the Sioux by tearing them down. They chased the cattle from the plains. The buffalo loved the Sioux as much as the Sioux loved them. They protected our way of life for both buffalo and Sioux."

"But then there was war between the White man and the buffalo," Chief Slow Bull continued. "They came and built forts and shot the buffalo as fast as they could, but still they kept coming. The soldiers alone were not enough to hold the buffalo's might. Then the Whites came with hunters who killed the buffalo only for their skins and left the rest to rot on the plains. They piled hides on their wagons and took them to the iron horse to carry them east, where they were to become the latest fashion accessories of the rich White men. As the buffalo has diminished, so has the Sioux, for our fates are sealed together. Tonight, we honor our buffalo brothers and prepare for the great chase tomorrow. May all play a part in the dance that brings the great herd up onto the plains before morning." With that, Chief Slow Bull retired to the fire and stood with the tribal elders.

The braves and the medicine men gathered in a circle around the fire and began beating out a slow rhythm on their drums. Mother Earth has a heart, and the Sioux drum helps her to find her heartbeat. The braves who had experience in the chase began to dance. They wore the revered trophies of past hunts, buffalo heads with horns, and strands of feathers flowing to the ground behind them. Their feet sought out the rhythm as they stirred up the dust. The women broke into song as the tempo of the dancing and drums increased its pace. Higher and higher leapt the flames as the braves threw on more wood, sending sparks up into the heavens where the Great Spirit could hear and see his people's call for help.

The full moon rose in the sky as the ceremony grew to a fevered pitch. The braves bowed down before the shaman and drank from the ceremonial cup. The shaman's herbal concoction—made of corn and honey that had fermented for weeks—gave the braves the energy they needed to stay up all night, gyrating and howling in dance.

Seeing the braves share the shaman's ceremonial cup reminded Remone of taking communion in the Catholic church. The shaman was like a priest performing blessings and healing his congregation.

The firewater took its effect on Remone as the Indians danced in their buffalo heads and shook their arms covered in trails of feathers. He saw colors swirling in the firelight. The drumbeat changed and started to sound more like the thunder of buffalo hooves. Remone strained his eyes as the dancing braves changed into their buffalo brothers and then back into braves. *So this is how they call up the herd,* thought Remone as he got a sense of the Sioux magic that they lived in every day.

He awoke to Pinchot shaking him. "Do you want to miss the glory of the hunt?"

Remone staggered into his teepee and pulled the hides around him to get a few hours' sleep before dawn.

At sunrise, the village was full of the sounds of braves preparing for the pursuit, excitedly gathering arrows into their quivers and checking the points to make sure they were sharp. Pinchot secured a spear in the leather tongs that held it on his horse.

Remone went to the campfire and poured himself a cup of tea from the holly leaves that the other braves were drinking. "What says the great hunter Remone? Is he ready for the chase?" Pinchot asked.

The shaman answered for Remone, "White brother will remember this day as long as he continues to draw breath. This day, he becomes Sioux!"

"This day, I hope to make you proud that you have accepted me into your family. Let my arrows fly true to their mark," Remone said as he plucked his bowstring.

"I have taught little brother well the way of the Sioux. He will make us proud and our bellies full of buffalo meat." Pinchot smiled as he released his horse from the tree and threw himself onto his horse's back.

Remone followed, jumping on Little Wing as Chief Slow Bull blessed the hunt. "Go with speed and may the Great Spirit protect you during the chase."

The braves galloped down from their campsite onto the open plain where they hoped to find the herd. Remone rode beside Pinchot and Looking Elk.

All at once, Black Wolf and his friends rode up to join the hunt. Black Wolf pushed his steed over into Remone's horse. "Why does white dog ride with true warriors?"

Pinchot placed his horse between Black Wolf and Remone. "His place will be that of true Sioux brother. He will earn his place in the tribe."

"White dog taints the hunt. Many things can happen during the chase!" Black Wolf yelled as he turned his horse and bolted ahead of the others.

Remone and Pinchot slowed their horses to distance themselves from Black Wolf and his companions.

The tribe climbed a bluff to search for the bison. The plain was one where the herd had eaten the grass of the prairie in great numbers before. But there were no buffalo to be found. Their scout, Looking Elk, moved in front of the other braves and searched the horizon, shading his eyes from the rising sun. Then he pointed north toward a grove of trees.

As they approached the grove, Looking Elk bounded down from his horse and sniffed the ground. Pushing over a buffalo turd, he said, "The big bulls have been here. They have moved on, we will follow," as he motioned to the west.

The tribe rode on in the direction of the mountains. The hills leading up to the mountains were rough and rugged, but there was one easy pass through which the buffalo and the Lakota Sioux might enter the hills. Every year thousands of buffalo spent the winter in the hills, in the place called Gate of the Buffalo by the Sioux.

It was at Buffalo Gap that they found the herd, heads down grazing on the winter grass. Some of the younger braves could not control themselves and started yelling when they saw the size of the herd. The buffalo stopped their grazing and started moving. The running bulls picked up momentum as they galloped into each other, nudging their shoulders into the smaller cows and snorting at them to get out of the way. The braves pursued what had turned into a full-fledged stampede, running up the hill and on through the pass.

The excitement was contagious as the chase quickened. Arrows flew and some of the slower buffalo were the first to fall. Because of the narrowing of the pass, the braves had to be careful not to get in the way of the stampede. Remone and Pinchot drove their steeds hard to get to the front of the herd. They could see some of the bigger buffalo running ahead of them. Then he saw him. Leading the herd was the largest bull Remone had ever seen. The bull zigzagged from left to right to dodge the arrows as he led the herd away from the screaming braves. His coat was covered with dusty sweat and the froth of his nostrils. But Remone could see the distinct hues of purple in his thick dark coat of fur that made him stand out from the other bulls.

Straining to keep his eye on the prize, Remone struggled to see through the dust. Urging Little Wing on, Remone drew an arrow from his quiver and readied it. He drew back on the bow but stopped just before he let it go. He just couldn't shoot the majestic Purple Buffalo.

Suddenly, Black Wolf crashed his horse into Remone's mustang, yelling, "White dog!" at the top of his lungs. Remone pulled back on his reins to slow Little Wing and let him pass. Pinchot urged his steed into Black Wolf and caught the full force of his whip across his face.

Pinchot reeled and lost his grip on Splitting Cloud as he slipped off the back of the horse into the middle of the oncoming buffalo.

Without hesitation, Remone drove Little Wing on using his steed as a shield to block the stampeding buffalo. Grabbing Pinchot by the arm and swinging him onto Little Wing's back, they galloped out of danger as the herd thundered past.

34

S KILL WITH THE BOW HAD been tested, and many bison had given their lives. News spread as they got closer to their encampment by the river. They had found the herd, and the tribe would not go hungry. Mothers and fathers, maidens and old men all came out to cheer the returning hunters.

The work of skinning the hides and drying the meat into jerky would soon begin. But tonight, they would celebrate the braves who had done their part in the chase. One White man would be honored, recognized for his contribution in saving the life of one of the tribe's leaders.

The moon had risen in the sky as the tribe gathered around the fire. Chief Slow Bull presided over the ceremony.

"When Pinchot pulled the White man from the river," Chief Slow Bull began, "I was one of those who did not welcome him here. Because of other White men I had known, I doubted that he could learn our ways. I expected him to flee our world and return to the Whites. But he has faced many trials and continues to earn his place among us today!"

The Indian celebrants cheered. Remone choked up as he smiled back at the chief.

"Now he has saved one of our own." Then the chief spoke directly to Remone. "I am pleased at the journey you have undertaken."

"What journey would that be?"

"The journey you are making to become a real human being. I hope you will finish your quest and become a great soul. You have chosen not to look upon your life as other Whites do. They seek only to plunder this world for their gain. I believe you are here to grow wiser by seeing through our eyes. By living the Sioux way, you will be forever changed."

"I am one who is unworthy to be called Sioux, but the darkness of my eyes has been lifted. I have seen the errors of my way and seek to redeem myself from the past."

"Because of your actions in the hunt," Chief Slow Bull said, "you have truly earned your place in the Lakota tribe. We will honor you as brother this night."

Slow Bull took red paint and rubbed it in a line from Remone's cheekbone to his chin. Then he pushed back his hair and drew an eye on his forehead.

"Now his inner eye is opened, his light will shine through the darkness. From this time forward, his Indian name will be Mowa Nambe, Shining Light. Remember, it is not with knowledge that one climbs the ladder of enlightenment, but it is through learning wisdom that the journey is completed."

"I welcome you, my brother Mowa Nambe," Pinchot said as he embraced Remone. "I was your teacher and protector, now it is you whom I owe much."

The shaman took Remone by the shoulders and looked deeply into his eyes. "Far have you come in your travels. Long may the turtle be your guide."

The buffalo cooking pots were full of the day's hunt. A pleasant aroma filled the air. At every teepee, there was a flurry of activity as they prepared for the night's festivities. A late fall sun set behind the trees on the distant pine-covered mountaintops, casting a reddish glow over the village. All was well. The only one missing from the activities was Black Wolf, gone from the village to escape the tribe's scorn.

35

A s Remone slept, he dreamed of the buffalo hunt and the events that had transpired that day. He awoke and thought, *I must tell someone what I saw.* He sensed that there might be jealousy and doubt among the tribe, so he waited until he and Pinchot were alone.

"I have seen the Purple Buffalo, he is real."

"Why would the Purple Buffalo reveal himself to you, a White?" Pinchot questioned. "I rode right next to you and never saw the great bull."

"I only tell you this as my friend, Pinchot." But Remone could still see the doubt in Pinchot's face.

"I must be about my work," Pinchot said as he excused himself, leaving Remone to his thoughts."

Remone started kneading one of the buffalo skins that had been brought back from the hunt. He went down to the creek to look for a bigger stone to use. He didn't mean to eavesdrop or hide, but as he stooped to look for the right-sized rock, he heard Pinchot and the shaman talking as they walked.

"Do not question the ways of the Great Mystery, Pinchot," said the shaman as he reprimanded him. "None of us know his secret workings. Maybe he seeks to use Remone as his messenger."

"But I was riding *right* beside Remone in the herd of buffalo and never saw anything except Black Wolf and his whip."

"I, too, have never seen the bull, but I believe he exists," the shaman said. "For generations, our people have told the legend."

"I have never questioned White brother. He has saved my life, but this is hard to accept."

"Give this time, I will talk to Remone."

The shaman sought out Remone. "I must talk with you, let us go down by the river's edge where only our ears will hear."

"Is this about what I told Pinchot?"

"Yes, he told me that you have received a vision."

"Well, I don't know about a vision."

"How could it be anything but a vision from the Great Mystery. You have already trudged a hard path. He has chosen you who has transformed himself into a Sioux. See that you keep an open ear to hear the message the purple bull has for you. Watch for him to enter your dreams."

"But why me?"

"Because you are to be an example."

"An example to whom?"

"You can be an example to Red man and White man alike. Just see that you tell no one else that you have been shown favor, having been embraced by the Great Spirit in this way. Keep this in your heart," the shaman said, touching his chest. "Draw power from it in your time of need."

The shaman went back to Pinchot. "I think the Great Mystery has given Remone his vision of the Purple Buffalo because he needs to continue on his path. Do not harden your heart against him; Remone is like an unfinished carving in the Great Spirit's hands."

36

THE FALL RAINS HAD COME to the village on the river. The air was colder with a hint of winter to come. Squirrels hurried about their work of storing nuts in the nests they had built. The three seasons that Remone had been with the Sioux had passed quickly.

"It is going to be a cold winter," Pinchot said as he watched the squirrels.

"How can you tell?" asked Remone.

"Look at the number of acorns that have fallen."

"Can you really tell from that?"

"The Great Spirit takes care of his children," said the shaman. "Yes, even the squirrels do not escape his gaze."

"It will be a long winter. Maybe one needs a woman to keep him warm," Pinchot said, laughing as he elbowed Remone.

"Yes," Chief Slow Bull came to attention and asserted as if on cue. "It is time for Remone to choose a wife."

"Now that you are Sioux," said Pinchot "You should look upon the beauty of our people and choose one to draw warmth from."

"First, we must build Remone a new teepee. One that smells better." The shaman laughed. "Larger and ready to handle many papooses."

"You have planned my fate?" said Remone, not sure how he felt about the whole idea.

"It is a good thing," Pinchot said. "We will show you the customs of courtship."

"The father thinks he decides who his daughter will marry," said the chief.

"But it is really the mother who tugs at the reins," said the shaman. "They like to see their daughters married."

"Both like to receive gifts." Chief Slow Bull nodded his head in agreement with the shaman.

The weeks that followed became like a series of auditions with mothers parading their daughters in front of Remone. The maidens of the tribe were not allowed to be alone with a man, but bringing samples of their cooking to Remone gave the mothers an excuse to bring their daughters together with a man under their watchful eye. "See how well Chumani cooks, one would not go hungry with her recipes."

Talutah, an older maiden, appeared with her mother around the communal fire. She was shy, and her mother did all the talking. "Talutah has made something for Remone to keep him warm in the cold months to come. See how skilled she is with her quillwork."

"I am unworthy of such a fine gift," said Remone as he held the shirt in his hands.

Another mother appeared with her daughter. "Look what my Kimela has made for you. A talisman. Look at her beadwork. My daughter would make someone a good wife."

It seemed to Remone that the giving of gifts worked both ways. But Remone grew tired of the attention. He retreated into the woods to escape the interest that the village was suddenly paying him. He worried he would offend the mothers and fathers of these Sioux maidens. He did not feel any attraction to any of the girls. The only maiden he felt anything for was Amber Moon, but she was spoken for.

Just two days ago, Dancing Bear had ridden into the village holding the reins of a fine horse next to his. He rode up to Big Elk's teepee and presented the horse to Amber Moon's father.

Remone tried to push her image from his mind. Then as he was walking the path back to his teepee at dusk, Amber Moon stepped out of the shadows of her teepee wearing a large buffalo blanket. *It is still warm*, thought Remone, *why is she wearing such a heavy coat?*

Then as she drew closer, she dropped the coat to show a very revealing outfit, buckskin shorts, the type of clothing a young maiden would sleep in but not wear outside. "Remone, please do not make me marry Dancing Bear, for I do not care for him," was all she said before she retreated back into her teepee.

But the effect on Remone was instantaneous. He had to step up his game. He went to Pinchot, seeking help.

"I need to find a suitable gift to present to Big Elk," said Remone.

"Yes, I thought Amber Moon had eyes for you, but you have a rival," said Pinchot.

"That is why I have come to you seeking help," said Remone. "I heard of Dancing Bear's gift. I need to come up with one that is better to win the favor of Amber Moon's father."

"Yes, we will have to improve on the gift Dancing Bear offered to Big Elk, as is our custom. We have raided the Crows' horses many times, and now they are too few. I know a place where the horses run free, but it is two days' ride from here. We will also have to train the horses to obey our touch."

Pinchot and Remone rode northwest to scour the plains, looking for wild horses. The terrain started to change on the second day. They left the lush green woods of the Black Hills for the bland wheatgrass of the plains. Then they reached the small hills and buttes where Pinchot said he had seen the horses before.

"I have seen the horses from a distance, many fine Appaloosas and spotted palominos," said Pinchot. I could tell there were mares from the young colts following the herd. We will have to choose the ones that will make a good gift."

"I hope we can find an Appaloosa that will make a good steed for Big Elk," said Remone.

"Catching a horse is different from hunting deer or taking buffalo for our nourishment. One needs to be gentle and avoid anything that would hurt the steed. See what I brought"—Pinchot held up a bundle—"White man's rope. I had to trade for it with beaver pelts. It will help to lasso the horses we choose."

"That will make it easier," said Remone. "Are you skilled with the rope?"

"Only a little," said Pinchot. "We may need to practice some. Look, there is the hill where they run."

In the distance, Remone saw a dusty sand covered hill, but no horses.

"We need to find the creek. There we will have water and can camp."

Pinchot and Remone gave their horses time to rest as they gathered firewood and set up camp. They shared the pipe as they discussed their plan of action.

"When we find the horses, we will need to separate them and drive them uphill to tire them out. That will make them easier to catch."

"That makes sense," said Remone as he drew on the pipe. Then he asked, "Have you ever thought about becoming one of the chiefs in our tribe?"

"I am a hunter, I commune with Wakan Tanka in nature and not in a teepee or council lodge. Being chief is a burden that would limit my freedom. I have all I want. My voice is heard among my people."

"You are highly respected among all the leaders of the tribe," said Remone. He asked no more questions. He did not want to offend his friend.

Pinchot jumped up and pointed. "Look, what do you see?"

Running across the plain, Remone saw the horses, close to fifty. He stood transfixed on the sight. A cloud of dust followed the beautiful ponies, colts, and mustangs. A white stallion led the herd as they charged on their way.

But Pinchot had already jumped on Splitting Cloud. "Come on!"

Remone leaped onto Little Wing and followed Pinchot. As they drew closer, Pinchot pointed to the right. Remone took his lead and rode his mustang toward the slower colts at the back of the herd. He looked and Pinchot already had his rope out and was spinning it in the air.

As he drew close to the horse he had chosen, Pinchot threw his rope in the air. It circled and dropped close to the horse, but the herd sped on while Pinchot retrieved his rope.

Remone rode over to Pinchot. "Almost!"

"Yes," said Pinchot as he hurried to roll the rope up under his arm. "Maybe we will try this another way. I was not being modest about my skill at roping."

Later after searching, they found the colts and mares playing in the river while the older horses stood as sentries protecting their young. Pinchot and Remone inched closer on foot to assess the location of the horses. They crouched on the ground as they came up with a plan.

"Look," said Pinchot as he pointed at the beautiful white stallion that stood guard.

"Beautiful," said Remone as they crept closer.

"I am going for the stallion," said Pinchot. "You move to the left to cut off his escape."

Remone jumped on Little Wing and rode to block the horse's retreat. But their astute rival was not caught unaware. Sensing the danger, he reared up on his hind legs and neighed loud enough to warn all the other horses before speeding away.

Pinchot was content to charge into the water and chase down an Appaloosa that was not fast enough in her escape. The water held her as Pinchot dropped the rope over her mane and pulled her into deeper water. Jumping on the mare's back, Pinchot let her buck until she had worn herself out.

"So that is how it's done!" said Remone as Pinchot emerged out of the river on the horse's back. They stopped to admire the colorful spotted coat of their new mare.

"It is good that you have seen how it is done, for I am not doing all the work!"

"She is a great prize," said Remone. "You have done well."

"Now that we know where they take their water, they will be much easier to find," said Pinchot on the way back to the camp. He rode the Appaloosa with Splitting Cloud tethered close behind.

As the sun went down on the pair of equestrians, Remone combed the long mane of the new addition to the band of horses they hoped to ride back to the village.

Cooking at the fire, Pinchot called out to Remone, "Be sure you have the highline tied tightly to the trees so our new mare does not escape."

"It is secure," said Remone. "She seems calm enough."

Pinchot took out his wooden flute and played softly. The notes carried pleasantly through the woods, mixing with the sound of the creek as it trickled over the stones.

"I have not heard you play the flute."

"I used to play more often when I was courting Chante. The maidens love to hear the sound. You must learn to play."

Remone joined Pinchot at the fire and asked, "How are we going to catch the white stallion?" knowing Pinchot would be the one with a plan.

"I have been thinking we may need to change our approach. We may need to make a net that we can drop on him. We will need to use something as bait to attract the wily white horse."

"How about a pear?" said Remone. "I saw some of the prickly pears growing down by the creek when I was getting water."

"That should work, we will have to start early in the morning to find the vines we will need to make the net."

The fire crackled as the two friends sat silently listening.

"I feel I have been transformed by my time here in the Sioux nation," said Remone.

"Just remember to achieve complete transformation, it is not enough to live. One must also die."

"Why must I die to be transformed?"

"It is the way it has always been for all people from those who first lived until our kind today. Through life we go through many transitions, transforming ourselves with each challenge. As we grow in wisdom, we transcend this life into the next one. Who can question the ways of the Great Mystery? He teaches us less through words and more through what we experience. Lessons that do not have to be memorized because they have been carved into our souls. Through the whole world, he teaches us. Through death, one is at last purified enough to stand before Wakan Tanka."

Most of the morning was spent weaving the net together. "Here, these vines should work well for our purpose," Pinchot said as he cut down several from the tree. "We will need to twist them together to give the net strength."

147

The net rose only four feet high, but they made it long enough to encircle their prize.

"Let us move our trap to the hill, there where he watches after the herd." Pinchot pointed. "We will wait for the stallion to leave."

The pair waited until the stallion went to cool himself in the river. "Tie that vine to the tree," said Pinchot. "You will have to hide here in the brush. I will signal you when to pull the net around the horse. I will come from behind and herd him into the net."

The stallion returned to his vantage point and shook the water from his mane. He watched the other horses as they played. Then he noticed the prickly pear and took three steps to pick it off the ground. Remone took the opportunity to close the trap as Pinchot waved him forward. He ran with the net circling the feet of the horse. Pinchot rode up on his horse and threw his rope over the stallion's neck and pulled it tight.

The stallion kicked with all his strength, trying to break Pinchot's grip, but the rope just pulled tighter. Remone dove headfirst into the dust to get out of the way of the flying hoofs. "I am afraid he is going to hurt himself, maybe the river will slow him down," Pinchot yelled as he struggled to lead the stallion down the bank and into the river.

Pinchot jumped on the stallion's back and pulled hard on the rope. The muscular horse snorted and snapped his teeth at his unwanted passenger. He bucked as hard as he could, rising out of the water on his hind feet. Pinchot continued steering him with the rope into deeper water until it was up to the horse's head. Still, he fought down to his last bit of strength. But the stallion finally tired.

On Little Wing, Remone joined Pinchot down at the riverbank. "The fire has gone out of him," Remone said to Pinchot as they brought the horses out of the water.

"Yes, he put up a good fight," said Pinchot. "A very impressive steed. We have done our work here. Let us go back to the campsite and rest."

The whole village turned out to see Remone and Pinchot's return. Word had gotten out from one of the hunting parties who had seen the white stallion. Braves looked on with envy, while Pinchot watched from a distance as Remone proudly paraded the two horses up to Big Elk's teepee.

Big Elk came out of his lodge and greeted Remone. "What a fine pair of horses," he said as he rubbed the stallion's mane.

"They are yours," said Remone.

"Let us smoke the pipe," said Big Elk as he opened wide the flap to his teepee.

"Yes, I knew you would be coming to see me," said Big Elk. "The shaman foresaw you would be bringing me a gift, but I did not think it could be such a fine offering. One that might be worthy of a daughter."

"Amber Moon *is* worthy of such a gift."

"Your words make me proud to have you as a son, but one horse would have been enough. Amber Moon has told me she cares for you. I want her to be happy."

Remone held his hand over his heart as he spoke the words he had rehearsed. "I want Amber Moon's light in my life, to guide me even on the darkest of nights. I promise to love and respect her."

"Your words ring true. Let us take a blood oath together," said Big Elk as he reached for his knife and opened a cut on his hand. Remone took his knife and did the same as they held their palms together, and Big Elk wrapped the cloth around their hands. As the blood soaked through the cloth, a sign for all the tribe to see, Remone could not hide his smile. *It worked! I have won Amber Moon!*

"With this blood oath, you will know I make a lifelong pledge of friendship to you," said Big Elk.

"And I make a pledge to always be there for you," said Remone.

"We are family now, let us tell the tribe."

Together they stepped out of the teepee and raised their arms high to the cheers of the village.

Remone sat outside of Amber Moon's teepee and waited for her to pass. "I do not know how to play the flute, but I have made a gift for you. An arrowhead in the shape of a heart to show I am giving my heart to you." Carved out of black glass obsidian, it sparkled in the light as Remone placed the necklace around her neck.

"With your arrow, you have smitten me."

"Do you remember when you bandaged my hand?" asked Remone.

"Yes. I never thought you would become so skilled with the chisel."

"I also have a gift for you," said Amber Moon. "Let me get it." She emerged from her teepee carrying buckskin pants. "I made these for you. See the turtle, your animal totem, on the legs."

Remone held the pants up to the fading sunlight. The craftsmanship was meticulous with blue turtles against the background of the tan leather. "These I will wear proudly and tell all who see them who made my buckskin."

Amber Moon rested her head on Remone's shoulder as they sat watching the setting sun over the hills. The birds' voices called out a love song, more beautiful than any flute, as a gentle breeze swept through the village. Time seemed to stand still for the two of them. It was as if they were the only two people on earth.

A great week of feasting followed the announcement. Women and children of the tribe formed a large circle and danced all day and into the evening to the sound of the drums. The village helped raise a new teepee for Amber Moon and Remone. They took their friends and family to see their new lodging.

"More room and much sweeter-smelling than your teepee." Pinchot laughed as he inspected Remone's new lodging. "May your lives together run as long as the eagle circles the sky."

The shaman acted as the master of the ceremony and announced that the hour of the proclaimed marriage had arrived. Four braves spread a large blanket with each taking a corner and holding it high enough in the air for Amber Moon and Remone to step under. They marched through the village with the shaman leading the crowd.

"Let it be known to all that the White man Remone and Amber Moon, the daughter of Big Elk, now are one," said the shaman. "Let us welcome them into the tribe with much celebration!"

They circled the village four times with their message for all to hear before stopping at the new couple's teepee. The sweet smell of yarrow flowers filled the teepee, and a fire crackled inside. The moon was high when they left the young couple to know each other.

37

Wasco Springs

THE SHAMAN SCOOPED UP THE special ceremonial mud from the riverbank while Pinchot and the other braves threw more wood on the fire that they had built next to the river. The earth the shaman used had clay in it and was the same mud the women used for making pots. It had a different texture and adhesive characteristics that made it right for the shaman's purification ritual. Once he had filled the large bowl, he backed away from the fire. It was too hot to stand close, with flames rising six feet into the air, blazing so intensely that one was warm even in the cool air.

"On this night, we gather to celebrate life," said the shaman. "We revel in the four wonders of this world—earth, wind, fire and water."

The shaman disrobed by the heat of the fire and began covering himself with the mud. Each of the braves did the same, as did Remone and Pinchot until they were covered from head to toe in the dark mire. They began to dance around the fire chanting while the mud turned hard on their skin, firing the braves like the pots they made. They laughed at each other as the earth pulled the toxins from their skin.

"You look like a skinny black bear," Remone said as he pointed at Pinchot.

"We are all mud men now!" shouted Pinchot.

"Let us make our way to the sacred pools," said the shaman to the group.

The full moon lit up the woods. They walked to the Wasco hot springs that flowed down a hill and poured into a small reservoir that made it perfect for bathing. Steam rose from the water in the cool air, giving the tributary a surreal, almost dreamlike look.

The shaman raised his hands to the heavens. "You have been sealed with the earth, baked by the fire, blessed by breathing the air, and now purified in the sacred waters of Wasco Springs."

All was right in Remone's world. *I am changed forever and could never go back to the White man's way. This is the happiest I have ever been,* thought Remone as they ran back to the village through the cool air.

38

As Remone slept, he dreamed. Walking alone in the snow, Remone scanned the horizon and saw only the trees and mountaintops covered in white. But as he continued to trudge through the deep drifts, he saw something approaching him. Heaving his chest as he jumped up and down to move forward, he saw the Purple Buffalo come into view. Fear seized Remone as it drew closer, and he thought he might be crushed by the massive bison. But the bull stopped five feet from him, raised himself up, and bellowed loudly, a sound like an ancient horn. The sound was so loud it shook the snow from the trees and caused avalanches to cascade down from the mountain ridges. It sounded like he was announcing an event so that all would take notice. The Purple Buffalo snorted and coughed. His breath turned to ice, filling Remone's eyes in a cloud of frozen mist that blinded him.

Then his dream took him back to the village. A crowd had gathered in the center of the hamlet. Through the crowd came Chief Slow Bull. He looked older than the last time Remone had seen him. He carried something, but Remone couldn't tell what it was until he stopped before the communal fire. He raised a crying baby boy high over his head to the cheers of the braves and women of the village.

Remone awoke. He knew his dream meant something, but what?

In the morning, he found the Shaman Returns Again warming himself before the fire.

"I have had a dream that I do not understand," Remone confessed to the shaman.

"Tell me your vision," the shaman answered.

Remone recounted all that he had seen. The shaman took a puff on his pipe and thoughtfully explained, "It is simple. The Purple Buffalo heralds the birth of your son that is to be. He will be a great leader, a healer, and a religious man that all may draw strength from. He will guide us all when I am gone. I have seen this child in my visions as he has grown into a man. This birth is your purpose in having been here in the Sioux nation."

The shaman went back to his cooking, and a stunned Remone walked back to the teepee where Amber Moon still lay naked on the bed their love had built.

39

PINCHOT PICKED A PLACE TO teach the young braves their next lesson. It was a place in the woods where the cliff jutted out and provided shelter from the wind and rain.

"Today we will practice building fires," Pinchot said. "I will show you how to make a bow drill. Look for a piece of wood that you can use as a spindle." Pinchot held up his hands. "About this long and sturdy enough to start a fire with. Here we need to sharpen it to a point." Pinchot used his knife to shave the end of the stick. "We will save the shavings. They will serve as tinder to help start the fire. For the bow, you need a curved piece of wood as long as your arm. Tie the line around the bow like this. You will also need an earth board where you will start your fire." Pinchot picked up a piece of wood and dusted it off. "This should work. We just need to cut a notch out of it that the spindle can sit in." Using the knife, he created a hole that would secure the spindle.

"What if you cannot keep the spindle in the hole?" asked Tusca. "I have tried this before, and it kept coming out."

"Here I will show you how it is done. Hopefully this wood is dry, you just have to spin the bow." Pinchot put the spindle into position with the bow tightened and started to pull it back and forth. His years of doing this showed as the friction quickly formed a trail of smoke smoldering on the earth board.

"Now take the ember to the tinder, you may need to blow on it gently but not so hard as to blow it out," Pinchot said as he blew on the tinder to encourage a flame.

"If one way to start a fire does not work, try another. If it has rained, a bow drill may not work."

Pinchot knelt and pulled a rock from his pouch. "How many of you know what rock this is?"

"It looks like a piece of pyrite to me," said Remone when none of the boys spoke up.

"Yes, good, Remone. This works as a flint. Striking these two rocks together produces sparks. See!" The braves watched as smoke began to billow out of the wood shavings.

Soon they had a roaring fire. Pinchot sat down with his pipe next to Remone and the shaman. He exhaled the rich smoke. "Nicely done," Pinchot said to the pack. "We will practice building fires until you have mastered the different ways it is done. Better that I test you than the bitter cold."

"Mother Earth can teach us many lessons," said the shaman. "Some from which you can learn much about yourself."

"Yes, always watch the animals of the woods," Pinchot added. "They will tell us what the weather brings. See how the crow has retreated to his treetop nest? We must be about to have a heavy rain."

"Just as the bird senses the coming storm, we sense what is coming," the shaman said. "There is another type of storm the White man is bringing to our people. Death and disease follow him into our heartland."

"But if we stand together as a nation, we can stop the advance of the Whites," Pinchot said to the braves.

"Yes," said the shaman. "Once there was a cloud who asked the mountain. 'Which is greater, the mighty mountain or the drop of rain?' Then the mountain replied, 'You are but a drop of rain. I am a mighty mountain. You drop on me and disappear.' But together the raindrops stormed down on the mountain, washing it bare of trees and soil. In the winter, the rain turned to ice, freezing in the cracks of the mountain and breaking up the rocks. In the end, the mountain was turned to sand, and still the rain continued to fall. What does this teach us?" asked the shaman.

"The mighty mountain is the White man," said Tusca.

"Together we are strong," answered Chatan.

"Yes, very good," said the shaman. "Anything is possible if we work together."

40

THE WOMEN OF THE TRIBE were once again harvesting the corn and grinding it into a smooth flour that they could store and cook with. It was very necessary work but somewhat dirty. Amber Moon worked to get the maize out of her fingernails. The sun had risen to its noonday height in the sky and warmed the air, so Amber Moon said to Talutah, "Let us go and bathe in the river while it is still warm."

As they walked down the path to the river, Amber Moon sang a song. "In my special home, the baby will soon come, leaving us not alone."

Talutah sang along with her as they cheerfully rounded the bend to the river.

In their private place, they undressed and waded in.

"Oh, this water is cold," said Talutah as she hesitated only knee-high in the water.

"That is why you have to dive in," Amber Moon said as she plunged into the water headfirst.

"Ooohhh, that is cold," Amber Moon said.

Talutah continued wading slowly into the water, which was now up to her waist, still shivering as she made her way deeper.

Amber Moon took the yucca root and washed herself with it, working her fingernails to get them clean.

"I have been practicing my quillwork. Have you seen the new shirt I have been working on?" asked Talutah.

"You are so good with the quill. I want to see it when it is done. You should teach me your skill."

The two friends continued to bathe in the slow-running water of the Cheyenne when suddenly Amber Moon heard a noise. It was a hooting noise like an owl, but this sounded human. Amber Moon stood completely still as she listened.

"Who's there?" she called out, but no one answered.

"What is it? Talutah whispered.

"Oh, nothing. I just thought I heard something," answered Amber Moon as she continued bathing.

Then she heard something else. It was the sound the Sioux made for calling deer, which is produced by taking a leaf between the lips and blowing on it so it rustled in their mouth, making a kazoo-like sound. Talutah and Amber Moon stood perfectly still as they heard a stick break.

"Maybe it's a deer and maybe not, or it might be some of the boys from the village spying on us," said Amber Moon in a loud voice, hoping to scare them out of the bushes. She headed for the riverbank and picked up her clothes with Talutah close behind.

Then she saw him as he stepped out from behind the brush. Black Wolf! She recognized him immediately. She knew he hated Remone.

He approached her and grabbed the clothes out of her hand. "Why do you cover that which I came to see?"

Amber Moon slapped him across the face and grabbed her pants.

Black Wolf laughed. "You have laid with white dog. How can you deny me?" He grabbed her hair and wrestled her to the ground.

Talutah grabbed a large limb and broke it with all her might over Black Wolf's head. The stunned brave rolled off Amber Moon.

"Come on!" Talutah yelled as she grabbed Amber Moon's hand and pulled her to her feet. They ran as fast as they could back to the village.

"Help!" Talutah yelled as they drew closer. "Black Wolf is attacking Amber Moon."

The men of the village answered her call and ran to help. But Remone went berserk, fire flashing from his eyes as he leaped on Little Wing and rode like a madman up the trail to the river. He came upon Black Wolf scurrying down the trail, holding his head where blood flowed from his wound. Remone charged on his pony, kicking Black Wolf in the mouth, and rode over him with Little Wing. Diving off his horse onto Black Wolf, Remone struck him in the face over and over again with the fury of a rabid grizzly until the other braves pulled him off.

"Do not kill him. It is for the council to decide," said Chaska to Remone.

The blood was pouring from Black Wolf's mouth and eyes as Remone lunged at him. "You must pay for what you have done!" shouted Remone.

"We will take him before Chief Slow Bull," said Canowicakte as the braves restrained Remone and Black Wolf.

A council meeting was called. All the braves of the village filled the hall, even Black Wolf's friends, but they were silent given the gravity of Black Wolf's misdeeds. Chief Slow Bull spoke. "From the time the White man Remone joined us, there has been bad blood between him and Black Wolf. But Black Wolf has shamed our tribe with his actions. Since Remone and his wife, Amber Moon, have been the ones wronged, it is Remone's right to take his life in the circle of death."

The men cleared the hall, leaving a space in the middle of the lodge where they would fight.

"You can do this, I have taught you well," said Pinchot calmly to Remone. "Do not let him cut your legs, or you will not be able to stand and fight." But Pinchot was full of angst for his friend.

Pinchot and the chief tied Remone and Black Wolf's left hands together and placed in each adversary's right hand a large stone knife. Then at the signal from Chief Slow Bull, the dance began.

The braves blew their bone whistles as the men fought and the intensity increased. Splinters of rock flew as the knives clashed. They lunged at each other and quickly pulled away, and the fight raged as they yanked on the rope that bound their hands together. Black Wolf was the first to draw blood with a swipe of his blade across Remone's leg. Blood ran down his leg and filled his moccasin. But Remone answered with a slash across Black Wolf's forehead, splattering blood into the air. The blood ran into his eye as the two continued to lunge at each other and leap away from the stinging blades.

Black Wolf with a forward thrust met Remone's blade, but Black Wolf's little finger sailed through the air. Blood began to cover the ground as the men struggled. The rope of hair that held their left hands turned frayed and red.

Black Wolf wiped at his brow to see. Black Wolf was fast, but Remone was faster. His anger burned inside, giving him the edge. As Black Wolf swung with his right hand, Remone stabbed him in the side and kicked the knife out of his hand. Remone yanked Black Wolf off his feet with the rope that held his hand and jumped on top of him with his knife at Black Wolf's throat. In a moment of mercy, Remone yelled, "Surrender or die."

"Please spare my life," cried Black Wolf.

Remone looked up at the chief.

In Remone's moment of weakness, Black Wolf leaped for his fallen knife and swung for Remone, but Remone struck him in the face. Blood poured out of Black Wolf's mouth as Remone spun him around and grabbed his right arm. Remone pulled the knife from Black Wolf's hand and didn't hesitate a second time. He plunged the knife into Black Wolf's chest. He held him firm with his left hand and pushed the blade in as far as it would go.

Black Wolf opened his mouth, but his lips formed no words, just a gurgling noise as he exhaled his last breath and fell to the ground.

Chief Slow Bull rose from his seat. "Black Wolf brought dishonor to his name and shamed our tribe by his actions. Remone has carried out his sentence of death. Black Wolf's name is never to be mentioned in this village again."

The feud was over, and Remone had won—but at a cost. Remone quickly took a piece of rawhide to use as a tourniquet to stop the flow of blood down his leg. *How was Amber Moon?* thought Remone. *It had all happened so fast. Where is she? He must find her.*

Remone left the council hall to look for her. Remone pulled back the flap to their teepee and found Amber Moon crying as she lay facedown in their bed of buffalo skins.

Remone knelt beside her and rubbed her back gently. "I am here for you," he whispered to her.

"Black Wolf has been punished. I will always be here for you, Amber Moon. Always."

Amber Moon rolled over to face Remone and hugged him.

"Oh, you are hurt," cried Amber Moon.

"It is nothing. I was worried about you."

He looked at her tear-stained face and lay down with her. They held each other through the day and until the night had passed.

41

INCHOT WAS ONE TO TEACH through example a role model for his students. He tried hard to teach them the Sioux way. Learning the skills of the hunter was exciting to them. Other tasks were viewed more as drudgery, but these skills were also valuable lessons to be learned. On this day of early winter, Pinchot showed them how to care for a valuable source of food.

"See the leaves that have fallen from the acorn trees." Pinchot pointed. "They are asleep for the winter. Here gather the sticks and leaves," he said as he handed a large leather bag to Kiowa.

The braves nodded hesitantly and started filling the bag. Remone gathered a handful of sticks and walked to where Pinchot stood and dropped them in a pile.

Handing a shovel to Kiowa, Pinchot said, "Push the dirt away from the roots and tell me what you see."

"I see tree roots."

"Look closer," Pinchot said as he stooped down and scratched the soil with his knife. "See moth larvae, this tree is infected. This can damage the acorn crop. We must burn around the roots to destroy this blight."

The other braves gathered to participate in the lesson.

"We will set a fire around these roots." Pinchot struck his flints together, and the leaves began to smoke. "But just enough fire to kill the moths and not injure the tree."

The braves watched as Pinchot controlled the flames with a stick. "All the acorn trees in this grove need to have the moths burned from their roots now during the winter months. The fire cleanses the soil and releases food to make the trees grow stronger in the spring."

"Here I will start a fire around this tree," Kiowa volunteered.

"We did not create the earth," Pinchot explained to the young braves. "It is a gift we have been given, which is why we must take care of it."

"But how do we who are only men do this?" asked Tusca.

"Sometimes it is only the small things we do that, by doing them consistently, play a big part in the plan," said Pinchot. "By taking care of what we have, like the food we eat, we know it will be here for the tribe when we are no longer here. We do not cut down trees, for they are alive. We look for wood that has already fallen to the ground to warm our food and bodies when it is cold."

"But how do you learn the plan the Great Spirit has for you?" asked Chatan.

"Discover and use your talents," Pinchot answered. "Some will be good hunters, some will be good warriors, others, like the shaman, will be good at healing the sick. All can play a part."

"But how does one discover their talents?" asked Chippewa.

"Many times it is in serving others that one sees his talents," said Pinchot. "Practice and perfect your talents. If not used, you will lose what talents you have."

"I want to be a great chief," said Kimanche. "For I have the wisdom to guide the tribe!"

"Like when you lost your horse on our last hunting trip?" Tusca laughed.

All the boys laughed at Tusca's comment, knowing that Kimanche needed to practice tying better knots, another important part of their necessary education for survival in the vast classroom of the Great Plains.

"All of us do their part in the life of the village," said Pinchot. "The women play a large part in our survival. It is not cooking or quillwork alone that they do. How many of you have helped move boulders to repair the reservoir? In the spring, the women work to channel the flow of water from the basin to the corn they have planted. After the harvest, they burn the cornfields just as we are doing now to purify the fields. This helps the corn to grow in the spring. Always they save just enough corn so that it can be planted so there will always be a harvest."

"Except in the seventh year," the shaman added as he joined the group, "for as is our custom, in the seventh year, the field must rest. This is part of our law as taught to us by the Great Spirit."

42

The orbiting of the sun,
the moon pulling the tides,
the turning of the planet,
from day into night,
clouds slipping away,
like a sunny day,
can't stop their flight,
or the passing days of my life.

THE SHAMAN RETURNS AGAIN HAD grown old. His wisdom weighed him down like a peach too heavy to continue hanging on the tree but about to fall to the ground, ripe and ready to be harvested. As the shaman's physical stamina faded, his psychic powers bloomed to their full potential, and his ties to the spirit world grew stronger.

Many times, a mother would come to the shaman, saying, "My daughter is ill, she must have eaten bad meat or drunk bad water. Come quickly and see what ails her." The shaman would say, "Wait, let me consult the spirits," and put himself into a trance in which he would ask questions and get answers from the other side. Moments later, he would respond, "Your daughter is with child. The great Spirit is giving you a boy. He will come in eight moons."

Always he was right.

Other times he would hurry to a teepee, carrying his bag of medicine without being summoned but knowing that a brave had been bitten by a poisonous spider or snake. The brave, who in his pride had not yet sought help, was still much relieved to see the shaman had arrived with the remedy for his affliction. Constantly keeping watch over his children, he could see and care for them using his inner sight.

Yes, the shaman had mastered the skill of putting himself into a different state of consciousness at will. He dedicated his life to serving his people. This allowed him to commune with the spirits, drawing power from them and giving him sight beyond sight. Often through these altered states he had visions that foretold the future.

Remone and Pinchot returned with the shaman to the sacred site on the mountaintop known as the Great Spirit's home. The old priest leaned heavily on his staff as he pushed his way up the mountain. Clouds gathered on the horizon as the three friends gained altitude. The sky seemed to press down on them as they climbed. Upon reaching the summit, the shaman breathed heavily leaning on a tree and said to Remone, "Pull the sage pouch from my tote sack. We must honor the Great Spirit here in his home." The shaman motioned to a bowl with ashes in it.

The shaman lit the sage and let it burn before turning it over. The sage smoldered as the pleasant fragrance floated in the air. The shaman sat on one of the boulders in the circle of the medicine wheel built years ago on the mountaintop.

"Pinchot, go get us some firewood. My bones feel the cold more than you with younger, thicker skin."

After Pinchot had walked into the woods, the shaman lit his ceremonial pipe, inhaled deeply, and handed it to Remone. "Have I told you of the vision I had of you, my White son? You will leave the Sioux nation and return to the White man's ways."

"No!" a defiant Remone exclaimed. "This can't happen. I will stay here forever. I will never leave what I have found."

"Remone, the dreams do not lie. I have seen you in the house of stone in which you worked with men and women in strange clothing. You will return to sell Mother Earth and fill your pockets with false wealth."

"No. I would never betray your trust in me and the lessons I have learned," Remone pleaded with the shaman.

"This is the path you will fall into *if* you do not gird yourself in the Sioux way and purge yourself of the greed that pursues you."

"This is the happiest I have ever been. I would never go back to my old ways."

Both the shaman and Remone ceased to talk as Pinchot, his arms loaded with wood, came up to the fire ring and dropped his load. "It looks like we might have rain." Pinchot pointed to the clouds gathering in the west.

"The birds fill themselves before the storm," said the shaman.

"Have some jerky," said Pinchot as he took out his bag and offered some to Remone and the shaman.

Flying en masse from trees to clearings, starlings had gathered on the mountaintop. They covered the branches and pecked the ground, looking for seeds.

"My days of leading the chosen people is at an end," said the shaman.

"No," said Pinchot. "The shaman will stay and guide his people with his steady hand."

"I have lived a life without regret, always a seeker of wisdom. My will and that of the Great Spirit have been as one. Soon I go to visit my ancestors and commune with the Great Mystery."

The sage had burned out as had the shaman's time. The last wisp of smoke vanished on the wind.

"Stay here while I pray to the Great Spirit," said the shaman. He stood and walked into the middle of the medicine wheel.

As they watched, he held his hands up to the sky and spoke. But they could not hear what he said. Slowly a murmur of starlings started flying around him, swishing their black wings as they reflected in the sun. Faster and faster the swirling funnel turned as more birds joined the column. The rustling of their wings became louder as they flapped harder. Pinchot and Remone stood spellbound watching the spinning circle. Then the shaman's figure grew blurred by the multitude of birds until the birds clouded the shaman from sight. The whirlwind of starlings rose in the air as the birds in flight continued to increase their speed. The shaman rose into the air, and suddenly he was gone.

Pinchot and Remone looked up into the sky. *Where had the shaman gone?*

"The blackbirds have whisked him away to the spirit world," said Pinchot.

Stunned, they looked at each other as the sky poured down its tears to mourn the passing of the great Shaman Returns Again. He had gone on to his rewards, but he had left the tribe with a big space to fill. Pinchot and Remone stumbled down the mountain in the downpour with one less member in their group. The walk down the mountain was a long one, and their feet were heavy but not as heavy as their hearts. But the shaman's last words to Remone troubled him even more.

43

THE FALL HAD PASSED, AND leaves that covered the ground were now covered in snow. Winter had set in. The cold that crept into one's bones stayed for the season. The buffalo had moved on to the winter ground and took with them the most dependable source of food. The supply of meat was running low, and the cooking pots were running empty. The tribal council asked the braves to bring back the hunt. Canowicakte, the hunter, Looking Elk, the scout, and Pinchot with his skill with the bow were chosen to lead the hunt.

"Remone will bring good medicine to the hunt," said Chief Slow Bull. "His will be a light in the dark of Winter."

"I will be glad to do my part for the tribe," said Remone.

These four it was agreed would leave the next morning, before dawn and after the moon had set in the sky.

The fire had burned out in Remone's teepee. Amber Moon wrapped her naked body around Remone for warmth. As he shivered in the dark, he heard his friends outside and remembered his promise to join the hunt.

"Stay with me and keep me warm," cooed Amber Moon.

"I will return after the hunt," said Remone as he kissed her cheek.

He forced himself to get up and pulled on his deerskin pants, boots, and his heaviest buffalo coat. Crawling out of his teepee, he saw his three friends laughing and sharpening their arrows.

Warming themselves one last time before they left the fire behind, Canowicakte asked, "Remone, how many arrows are in your quiver?" The hunters laughed.

"How many arrows?" answered a still half-asleep Remone. "Oh, none," he added as he realized it was empty.

"Remone is such a good hunter that he will just throw rocks to bring down his venison." Looking Elk laughed.

They made their way in the dark but were glad when sunlight warmed the trail. Looking Elk led the way as they grew silent, concentrating on the hunt. Walking down the path, the only sound was their footsteps crunching the ice. The four hunters turned to follow the creek bed where the saplings grew. The trail covered in snow was difficult to follow and slippery, so they moved forward carefully.

A light snow fell as Looking Elk motioned them off the path. Looking at Remone, he covered his lips with one finger, and with a "Shhhh," he pointed to the fresh tracks in the snow. Then he pointed to Pinchot and Remone motioning them to the left of the trail while he and Canowicakte continued to follow the tracks.

Following Pinchot, Remone tried to step lightly in his footprints to avoid making any sound that might spook their game. They worked to get further ahead of their companions and flush the deer in their direction.

The pace slowed as they worked their way through the thick underbrush downhill toward the river. Stepping on top of a large boulder, Remone slipped on the icy rock. He caught himself before he fell, but as he recovered, Remone sat still for a moment. From the top of the rock, he saw something moving through the trees.

Looking down to judge his next steps, Remone crept silently through the woods. Pinchot was nowhere in sight. He continued toward the grove where he had seen something moving.

He could hear the water moving under the ice as he got closer to the river. Remone found a clearing where he could see both sides of the bank. Down to the right he saw the doe! She was standing still, listening and sniffing the air like she sensed the danger. Remone stood still until she went back to eating the cottonwood bark.

Remone approached the doe, crouching as close to the ground as he could, using the brush as a cover. The doe was looking straight at Remone like she knew he was there. She started swishing her little white tail nervously. But at sixty feet away, Remone knew that even a skilled brave would have a hard time making the shot. He had to get closer.

Remone stayed perfectly still until the deer started eating again. He silently inched closer and took an arrow from his quiver. Aiming for just above the deer, he let the arrow fly. But as the arrow sailed, he realized he had not accounted for the wind. It took the arrow to the left of the deer, hitting a tree with a loud *thunk*. The doe leaped in the air and bounded farther down the riverbank.

Remone thought he might get a second shot and followed the deer. Carefully Remone closed the distance. He was lucky he could still see the deer, but he wondered, *Where was Pinchot?*

The doe had gone out onto the ice and was crossing the narrow space that separated her from the other side of the river. *I have got to move fast, or the doe is going to get away*, thought Remone as he reached for another arrow and stepped forward. The next sound he heard was the ice cracking as he realized his mistake. The ice gave way underneath him, swallowing Remone into the frigid flow!

He sank beneath the surface, and the weight of his coat grew heavier by the second as it soaked up water. Remone struggled to remove his coat as he kicked with all his might to get back to the top.

The strong current beneath the ice pushed him downstream. He separated himself from his coat and tugged his boots full of water off, but as he kicked his way up to reach the surface, he found a crystal ceiling above him. His lungs burned for air, but he had nothing to break the ice with. Then he remembered his knife tied around his waist. Could he get it in time? His hand shook as he grabbed the blade and smashed it into the ice once, twice. Then it slipped from his freezing hand. Remone watched as the knife, his only means of escape, sank to the bottom of the river.

Remone felt at peace. He didn't have any fight left in him and prepared to see the Great Mystery. He dreamed a dream he had had before. He was riding Little Wing faster than he had ever ridden the pony before on a path that grew more and more narrow until it was just a ribbon of light leading him up to the sun. He saw the face of Wakan Tanka. His smiling countenance welcomed him in; as he drew closer, the flames erupted, and fire exploded around him.

Remone felt the heat and smelled the burning flesh as he urged Little Wing on, riding the beam into the mouth of the Great Mystery. As the cosmos swallowed up Remone, he saw many things more clearly as his life flashed in front of him. It did not take an eternity to understand, only death.

44

B UT REMONE AWOKE TO LARRY and Jim, his camping buddies, pulling him out of the icy water and throwing him onto his back.

"Is he breathing?" asked Jim.

But Larry had already started doing compressions on his chest. Remone started to cough up water as Larry continued beating on his chest.

"Turn him over on his stomach so he won't choke," Jim said as he rolled him over and pulled him off the ground with both hands, trying to squeeze the water out.

"Come on, Remone," Jim shouted. Over and over, he repeated the motion until Remone threw up water. He coughed and opened his eyes.

"Whew!" said Jim. "That was scary. I almost thought we had lost you!"

"What made you walk out on the ice? Now you lost your rifle! Dumbass!" said Larry, admonishing Remone as they helped him to his feet.

"You are lucky we heard your yell," Jim said. "You were under for a couple of minutes I didn't know if we could bring you around."

At first, Remone was unable to respond as he struggled to maintain consciousness. Slowly he stuttered. "Where am I? Where's Pinchot?"

"Who?" asked Jim.

Remone coughed as hard as he could but was still having trouble clearing his lungs. "I am confused," Remone struggled to say. His eyebrows were caked in ice, and he ground his teeth to keep them from chattering. His coat was gone as he shook in the freezing cold.

"He must have been under longer than we thought," said Larry. "He's delirious. Come on and help me get him back up the hill to the fire."

They dragged him with his arms thrown over their shoulders, struggling up the hill. Remone was deadweight as his bare feet left a trail in the snow. Unable to talk clearly or recognize his surroundings, Remone fought to make sense.

"Where are your shoes?" Jim asked.

"I must have lost them in the river," Remone mumbled.

David was outside his tent making coffee when Jim exclaimed, "Look what we pulled from the river!"

"Oh my god!" David exclaimed as he ran over to help them. "Remone, are you okay?"

"I have to get some dry clothes," said Remone as he stumbled into his tent and put on the extra clothes that he had brought. *I am glad I brought extra boots, but I am still freezing*, thought Remone. He grabbed a blanket and collapsed with his feet next to the fire.

David offered Remone a cup of coffee. "Do you need an aspirin?" He handed him a container of Bayer, both of which Remone gratefully accepted.

Greg crawled out of his tent. "What the hell happened?"

In Remone's state of confusion, Larry answered for him, "Dumbass fell in the river and lost his rifle. He would have died if we hadn't heard his yell!"

Remone sat in dumb bewilderment, trying to thaw his feet out. The rest of the campground was full of activity with his friends preparing to go out hunting and packing gear away into their tents.

"Have some jerky," said Greg as he sat down. "Remone, you look like shit. Are you okay?"

"Yeah, I'm just whipped."

"Well, I'm going out hunting and wanted to make sure you were okay. You should just stay here and rest."

Remone nodded his head.

Greg got his rifle out of his tent and said, "I am going hunting!" giving Remone a thumbs-up as he headed into the woods.

Remone awoke in an empty campground as he slowly gathered his thoughts. Where had his Sioux brothers gone? He decided to look for them. Maybe he could find his way back to the village. He began walking along the ridge, distancing himself from the river and his near death.

As the snow began to fall again, he worried he might lose his own tracks. He reached a clearing where he could see the river and thought, *If I can find the trail we were on before I fell in the water, maybe I can follow the path back to the village.* He started down the slope but slipped and rolled down the hill. The snow broke his fall, but he lost his sense of direction.

Then his heart leaped in his chest. Smoke! Maybe it was his Indian friends? Remone began to run. *Thank God!* Thought Remone. *This has to be Pinchot, Canowicakte, and Looking Elk's fire. They are probably just resting and waiting for me to find them. I'll introduce them to my buddies.*

He followed the flumes of smoke in the sky back to its source and saw five tents, one his own. He had gone in a circle and realized it was the campfire he had just left. Collapsing to his knees and gasping for breath, he buried his face in the snow and prayed to the Great Mystery as he tried to hold onto the paradise he had come to love. *Please let me stay, I will do anything to stay here in the Black Hills.*

But then Remone was glad to have the warmth of a fire. His pants were wet from the snow. He threw more wood into the pit and rekindled the fire. He went back into his tent and found some food, still frozen, he could cook. His buddies were out hunting, and Remone had time to reflect. He tried to gather his thoughts from his foggy head.

Maybe it had all been a dream.

45

STARING OUT THE WINDOW OF the Suburban, he watched as the South Dakota landscape rolled past. Remone lost himself in thought. What had he just experienced? Where had he been for the past year? Or had it only been for a brief moment, only the minute he was in the river's grip? Maybe he had a near-death experience, but it all just seemed like a dream the farther they drove away from their campsite.

Remone fell asleep and didn't wake up until they stopped to drop Larry off at his house. Jim and Greg helped unload his camping gear as David asked him, "Hey, you doing okay? You've been awfully quiet. You didn't inhale too much water, did you?"

"No, I'm okay, just tired." He didn't want to tell David he was disappointed to be back, that all he wanted to do was remain with the Sioux. He felt like he had been interrupted from finishing his dream.

The group was silent as they dropped off Jim and Greg and headed for Remone's house. David helped him unload his camping gear. "Sorry about your rifle, tough break since it was brand new."

"Yeah, I'll get over it," said Remone. "I appreciate you driving. Do you need some money for gas?"

"No, this trip cost you enough," said David. "Are you going to work tomorrow?"

"I am afraid I don't have much choice."

"Well, I hope it's a soft landing. I'll catch up with you later this week."

"Yeah, thanks for everything. See you."

A soft landing, I wish, thought Remone while he brought his gear inside.

An exhausted Remone went to sleep early with a nagging anxiety already starting to eat at his gut. Just the thought of returning to work made him sick to his stomach.

The sunlight flooded through Remone's window as he awoke. Sucking down a second cup of coffee, he slowly drove to the West Des Moines ERA Real Estate office.

"Oh, Remone, I am glad you're back," said Stella. "You have some things to take care of and you have a ton of messages. And Mrs. Cooper and Mr. Gant want you to meet with them this morning."

The pit of Remone's stomach ached. *I need to call Mrs. Cooper and see if I can get this meeting canceled.*

Remone dug through the papers on his desk. *Where is the paperwork for Mrs. Cooper?*

"Stella, do you know what happened to the papers on the house at 1011 Autumn Circle?"

"Is that Mrs. Cooper's house?"

"Yeah, that's the one."

"Well, you left them back there next to the Xerox machine. I didn't think you wanted them, so I gave them to Mr. Gant."

"Oh no, you knew I was working with her," said Remone as he felt his blood pressure spike.

"Well, that's between you and him. I think he wants to give the listing to Sarah. You shouldn't leave your papers just lying around."

Sarah came into the office, looking stunning and wearing the highest high heels Remone had ever seen. "Hey, Remone, how was the camping trip? Did you bag the big deer you were hunting for?"

"No, I lost my new rifle and just about drowned. It was an adventure, but I'll have to tell you about it later."

"Remone, I need to see you and Sarah in my office right now," said Gant over the intercom.

Oh boy, here it comes, thought Remone as he and Sarah went into Gant's office.

Mrs. Cooper frowned at Remone as he came through the door.

"I am sorry you had to call me Mrs. Cooper and that Remone handled your property so poorly," said Mr. Gant.

"Well, me too," said Mrs. Cooper. "Remone has just wasted my time."

"That's why I wanted to introduce you to Sarah. She is our top salesperson."

"Good to meet you," said Sarah as she shook Mrs. Cooper's hand.

"Well, it's about time," said Mrs. Cooper.

Mr. Gant got up and shut his door. "Well, I didn't want to do it, but you made me do it, Remone. I am putting you on probation. Fill out this paperwork."

After being browbeaten by Gant for close to an hour, Remone didn't care; he just wanted to get out of Gant's office. He got the listing he had written up for Mac and Myra Sims. The pictures of the house looked good. He just needed to go over some things to do to the house to get it ready to show. *Yeah, now would probably be a good time to turn in this listing.*

"Remone, have you been sandbagging me?" said Mr. Gant over his phone speaker. "I guess putting you on probation was a good idea."

"Well, I had been working on this listing for a while."

A full moon cast light through the trees and onto Remone's dashboard and seemed to follow him home. The glowing celestial body reminded Remone of Amber Moon's beautiful eyes.

Remone kicked the sheets off his bed as he struggled to get to sleep. "Where did you go and why did you leave me?" Amber Moon's voice called to him through his dreams. The memory of her pierced his soul, but was it real? Had the year in the Dakotas lasted a year or only minutes? The more he thought about it, the more Remone felt he had experienced much more than a dream but rather a near-death experience, which took him to another world to teach him before returning him to this one.

I can't sleep, Remone sighed as he got out of bed. *I may as well clean the house.*

He pulled socks and shirts from his backpack, and there it was! The deerskin pants he had on when he fell into the river, the leather tassels hung from the side seam. Remone held them up to the light and looked at the turtle design that Amber Moon had put along the inseam. You couldn't buy these at Over the Mountain Outfitters. It was proof! Proof that he had been somewhere real! An excited Remone tried to make sense of it. It was not until the wee hours of the morning that he fell asleep.

The next day, Remone was lucky enough to have a two-o'clock appointment at the office. Connie and Emanuel Satterfield had their cute little three-year-old daughter, Sophie, with them. She patiently waited while they filled out their agreement.

"Look what I have for you," said Remone as he handed her a coloring book they kept around the office for kids.

But Sophie clung to her stuffed toy and curled up defensively in her chair.

"What's that you got there, Sophie?" asked Remone as he looked at her stuffed toy.

"It's my turtle. He's my friend, he tells me stories at night when Mommy and Daddy are asleep."

"Oh, that's cute," said Remone.

"I have a question," said Connie. "Suppose we decide we're not going to buy a house from you. There is no contractual obligation if we decide to work with another real estate agent, is there?"

Oh no, thought Remone. *I hate when they ask that.* "No, ma'am, this just states that my obligation is to work with you in your best interest and not on behalf of the seller. I've got some great listings to show you."

In the parking lot, Connie frowned when she saw Remone's Camry. "Emanuel, you sit up front with Remone. I'll sit in the back with Sophie," she said as she crawled into the back seat.

Three hours later, Remone remembered the saying, "Buyers are liars," as they had not seen any homes that were up to their high standards.

"I don't know, Remone. I think we are just going to have to think about it," said Connie. "Just take us back to the office for now. I have to go home and get dinner started."

It was a rapid exit from the real estate office, without the young couple even coming inside. They just jumped in their car and hurried off.

Dang, I'll call them back tomorrow and get them to go out looking again. At least I got a listing today.

Going into the office after five was a rarity for Remone, but he had something he wanted to check. The office was dark inside. Clicking on the lights and going past the conference room, he heard something and looked in. There was nothing there except Sophie's stuffed turtle leaning up against the leg of the table. Remone scooped up the toy and carried it to his office. *Maybe I can use this to get back in with the Satterfields.*

Remone clicked on his computer and started looking at homes in the same neighborhood that Mac and Myra Sims lived in. *This one looks good. I wonder how much they want for it.*

Softly he heard it like it was being whispered to him, "Remone, listen."

Remone looked around his office. *There's no one here. You just imagined it.* Then he looked at the turtle. *Oh no, now you're just imagining things. But who had moved the stuffed toy? That's not where I put it.*

Remone left the office and started on his way back home. *I am losing it, seeing and hearing things. I've got to go home and have a beer.*

After a six-pack and an evening of changing channels on the television, Remone called it a night. Falling back into his old ways, Remone had taken to drinking excessively to deal with the stress of the real estate office. He spent a restless night trying to go to sleep.

As he drifted off to sleep, a visitor entered his dreams, his friend the turtle.

"I am your animal totem, Remone," said Many Faces. "It is hard to get a message to you. I will always be here to help you, but you must find the time to listen. You are not going to be able to change if you are at the same job with the same people doing the same thing."

"What is it that you want with me?" Remone heard himself ask in his dream.

"Only to ask you a question," answered the turtle. "You have been shown the keys to escape your prison. Why do you remain?"

Remone awoke from his dream and got out of bed. He spent the rest of the night pacing through his house. By morning, he knew what he must do. As the sunlight flooded his room, he dressed for work. He was going in a little bit early this morning.

Getting to the office before Mr. Gant and Stella, Remone taped an envelope to Mr. Gant's door and left.

Mr. Gant arrived at the office and opened the note. "Remone," called Mr. Gant over the intercom. "Remone!"

But Remone did not answer. He was driving his little Camry west with his map book in the passenger seat next to him opened to South Dakota.

"Stella, have you read this note?" Mr. Gant asked.

"I am going in search of the Purple Buffalo, signed Remone," read Stella with a puzzled look on her face.

"What does that mean?" asked Mr. Gant.

THE END

About the Author

BORN AND RAISED IN BIRMINGHAM, Alabama, Chuck's extensive knowledge about the lifestyle and religious beliefs of Sioux Indians gives a message to the reader and gives them pause to think. A communications graduate of Auburn University, Chuck's background includes copywriting for radio and television over a span of forty years.

Milton Keynes UK
Ingram Content Group UK Ltd.
UKHW040117170324
439511UK00001B/55